MONTVILLE TWP. PUBLIC LIBRARY
90 HORSENECK ROAD
MONTVILLE, N.J. 07045

MORRIS AUTOMATED INFORMATION NETWORK

0 1021 0233097 8

S0-BAT-276

JFICTION
Sando
Sandor, Steven

Playing for Keeps

Montville Township Public Library
90 Horseneck Road
Montville, N.J. 07045-9626
973-402-0900
Library Hours
Monday   9 a.m.-9 p.m.
Tuesday   9 a.m.-9 p.m.
Wednesday   9 a.m.- 9 p.m.
Thursday   9 a.m.- 9 p.m.
Friday   9 a.m.- 6 p.m.
Saturday   9:30 a.m.- 5 p.m.
Sunday   1 p.m.- 5 p.m.
see website   www.montvillelibrary.org

PLAYING FOR KEEPS

Steven Sandor

James Lorimer & Company Ltd., Publishers
Toronto

Copyright © 2012 by Steven Sandor

All rights reserved. No part of this book may be reproduced or transmitted in any form or by any means, electronic or mechanical, including photo-copying, or by any information storage or retrieval system, without permission in writing from the publisher.

James Lorimer & Company Ltd., Publishers, acknowledges the support of the Ontario Arts Council. We acknowledge the financial support of the Government of Canada through the Canada Book Fund for our publishing activities. We acknowledge the support of the Canada Council for the Arts, which last year invested $24.3 million in writing and publishing throughout Canada. We acknowledge the Government of Ontario through the Ontario Media Development Corporation's Ontario Book Initiative.

The Canada Council | Le Conseil des Arts
for the Arts | du Canada

ONTARIO ARTS COUNCIL
CONSEIL DES ARTS DE L'ONTARIO

Cover image: iStock

Library and Archives Canada Cataloguing in Publication

Sandor, Steven, 1971-
    Playing for keeps / Steven Sandor.

(Sports stories)
Issued also in electronic formats.
ISBN 978-1-4594-0067-2 (bound).--ISBN 978-1-4594-0066-5 (pbk.)

    I. Title. II. Series: Sports stories (Toronto, Ont.)

PS8637.A547P53 2012   jC813'.6   C2012-900323-9

James Lorimer & Company Ltd.,   Distributed in the United States by:
Publishers   Orca Book Publishers
317 Adelaide Street West,   P.O. Box 468
Suite 1002   Custer, WA USA
Toronto, ON, Canada   98240-0468
M5V 1P9
www.lorimer.ca

Printed and bound in Canada.
Manufactured by Friesens Corporation in Altona, Manitoba, Canada in February 2012.
Job #72986

For my wonderful wife, Noelle, and our little teammate, Tate. Noelle has supported my efforts, putting up with late-night writing sessions and a scattered schedule. Tate, may every dream you have come true.

CONTENTS

1 DOUBLE TROUBLE

The Pelletier twins, Rejean and Ronnie, raced across the centre line. If not for the different numbers on their backs, it would have been impossible to tell the two Morinville forwards apart.

Ronnie smacked the puck across the blue line, and it cracked as it hit the blade of Rejean's stick. The Barrhead defenceman skated backwards, trying to guess Rejean's next move. As the defenceman hesitated, Rejean took off in a blue and white flash, driving towards the goalie.

The goalie came out of his net, trying to cut off the angle. Rejean raised his stick as if he was going to shoot the puck right *through* the netminder. But, at the last second, he flicked a pass towards Ronnie.

Ronnie simply directed the puck into the open net.

The crowd around Branko Stimac erupted. Branko lost sight of the ice as the people in front of him rose to their feet. He didn't bother getting up from his seat. He didn't join the *chump-chump-chump* of applause from fans whose clapping hands were muffled by their mittens.

"Wow, isn't this exciting!" said Branko's friend, Scottie, as he flipped his camera over so he could look at the little screen on the back. "I hope I got that."

"Not really," said Branko. "Ronnie and Rejean just scored another goal in a game we all knew they were going to win."

The goal had just put the Morinville Warriors up 4–1. Ronnie had scored all four home-team goals. Rejean had set up all four.

Scottie hit the playback button with his thumb. "Darn. Looks like they're playing in a snowstorm. Branko, I wish I could stop this lens from fogging up. It's just too cold in the arena."

Branko and Scottie always made sure to sit in the row that was right under the heat lamps that hung from the ceiling, but still there was no getting around how cold it was. The mist seeped out of their mouths as they exhaled. And there was no escaping the smell — a mix of hot chocolate, coffee, and French fries.

"You know, you put a lot of effort into blogging about two guys who don't like you, Scottie. Do you remember when we came here for the public skate? The Pelletiers put a chair out for you! They told everybody you skated like a three-year-old!"

Scottie shook his head. His dad had told him that if he wanted to work for the paper, he had to "have thick skin." Which meant writing good things about people who didn't like you and not being afraid to criticize the people who did like you. It was messed up, Scottie thought, but his dad had run the town paper since before he was born, and it did just fine.

"You know what, Branko? That doesn't matter." Scottie raised the camera and pointed the lens towards the ice. "The Pelletiers might be famous one day. Heck, they knew Gretzky was gonna play in the NHL when he was what? Nine! People from all over the country visit my blog to see what the Pelletiers did!"

"I just don't get it. Why does everyone like hockey so much? You sit here shivering. The puck is so small you can't follow it. Everybody moves so quickly you can't read the plays. And, the guys only play a minute at a time. Now, soccer — *that's* a real sport! You have to stay on for the whole ninety minutes!"

"Oh, hey," said Scottie, lowering his camera. "You've got that tryout coming up, right?"

"Yes," said Branko. "It's tomorrow at eight a.m." Tomorrow he would try out to be the goalkeeper for Edmonton's top junior soccer team, the Selects. Tomorrow the years of driving to tournaments in Edmonton, Calgary, Red Deer, and Lethbridge would finally pay off. Tomorrow was going to be the biggest day of his life.

"Branko, can I write about the tryout in the blog? Put it on the newspaper's website!"

"Why? No one in Morinville would care."

The crowd *oohed* as one of Morinville's second liners knocked down a kid from Barrhead at centre ice. Scottie quickly brought his camera back up to his eye. "Darn! I missed it!"

The stands were packed. Parents hollered and clapped. Kids lined up at the concession stands, clutching loonies in their cold hands. On a Saturday night, the Ray McDonald Sports Centre — which most people still called by its old name, the Agriplex — was *the* place to be in Morinville.

Branko had moved to Morinville from Edmonton when he was five, but he still felt like the strange kid in town. In eight years, Scottie was the only real friend he'd made. Branko had tried to fit in with the other boys, but he couldn't join their conversations about the hockey games they had watched or their dreams of making it to the NHL. He had once tried to explain ice hockey in a letter to his grandfather, who had politely replied, "Ice hockey? Don't they play that once every four years at the Olympics?"

In Branko's family, soccer was everything. Branko's father, Josip, had played professionally in Croatia (then part of Yugoslavia) before the civil war, and he had started teaching Branko the game as soon as he could walk.

Scottie leaned forward as the Pelletiers hit the ice for another shift. A Warriors player slid the puck into Rejean's feet. Without missing a beat, Rejean kicked the puck towards his stick, caressing it on the blade as he hit the blue line. He streaked along the boards, around the Barrhead defenceman. He swooped behind the goal as his brother hit the slot. One quick pass, and Ronnie one-timed his shot through the legs of the goaltender.

The crowd roared again.

Finally, after what seemed like an eternity to Branko, the buzzer sounded. The crowd gave the Pelletiers a standing ovation as they skated a post-game victory lap. Branko got up, too — not to clap, but because he wanted to leave his seat and go someplace warm.

Branko filed out to the lobby with the crowd, while Scottie headed down the stairs to the dressing-room area to get some quotes from the Pelletiers.

Branko waited at the main concession for his friend as the fans slowly made their way out into the frigid night air. Scottie arrived just as the concessionaires were closing up for the night.

"Sorry, had to get all the interviews done. You didn't have to wait for me."

"What would be the point in rushing home?" said Branko, shuffling his boots. "I didn't sleep much last night and I know I won't sleep tonight. I'll just lie in my bed and stare at the ceiling, worrying about the tryout. So I may as well be here."

Scottie laughed. "I guess that's sort of a compliment. That you'd rather hang out with me than stare at a ceiling."

2 THE TRYOUT

Josip climbed out of the truck, stretched, and grabbed an equipment bag out of the backseat. With his free hand, he banged on the side of the pickup's cab. "C'mon, Branko! Time to go!"

Branko climbed out of the passenger seat. He stretched, then yawned.

"Wake up, son," said Josip, his heavy accent making his *w* sound like a *v*. "I have your bag. Look, you shouldn't have gone out last night to watch that silly hockey match. You need to get sleep before practice."

The sun wasn't up yet. *That's Alberta in February,* thought Branko. *You have to wake up before the sun. You have to eat breakfast looking out at the moon through the kitchen window.*

"Dad, it's not even seven-thirty yet," said Branko, stifling another yawn.

"You should always be early for practice. Especially for a team like the Selects," said Josip, already walking through the skiffs of snow in the parking lot. "The invitation said you must be on the field at eight a.m. Not 8:01. Coach Muller will send you home if you are just one minute late."

Josip and Branko had spent a little less than an hour driving south on the highway from Morinville to Edmonton. Now, they walked towards the indoor soccer centre. It was still far too cold to play outside.

Branko walked through the doors of the soccer centre and took a deep breath. Even though this was the first practice of the day, the smell of sweat was heavy in the air. It was in the walls, the turf.

Coach Muller was already standing in the middle of the field, clipboard in hand. Branko's father shook the coach's hand. Josip wore a shiny blue jacket that had been given to him when he'd first made the NK Osijek team as the third-string goalkeeper. It was the same jacket he wore when he got to be the backup, and he kept it after he got the starting job.

Josip beckoned his son over.

"So this is Branko," said Coach Muller. "I heard about what you did with Sturgeon County last year. Maybe you'll be as good as your dad was."

"Did you ever see my dad play?" Branko asked.

"Just after he and your mom came to Canada, the Edmonton semipro team offered him a tryout. He made it. I was on that team, too. Fullback."

"Really, Dad?"

"Yes, before you were born," said Josip. "It wasn't

much money and the bus rides were long. And it got in the way of my regular job; I had to ask for too many days off. I quit when your mama was pregnant with you."

"Okay, enough with the history lesson," Coach Muller said. "Go get changed, Branko."

As Branko walked into the dressing room, he saw about forty other kids packed in there. Branko knew that half of them would be cut before the next practice. There were hundreds of other players who would have loved a chance to make the team — but the Selects offered tryouts on an invite-only basis.

"Hey, you . . . are you the kid from Morinville?" came a voice from the bench.

"Yes," replied Branko, looking around.

"I heard your dad called Coach Muller dozens of times to get you this tryout."

Branko found the voice. It came from a boy who was slipping on a pair of goalkeeper's pants. Branko hadn't expected this. He'd thought the other kids would be like him — quiet and nervous.

"Who are you?" Branko looked at the boy. "And my dad doesn't have to do anything for me. I won every game I played for the Sturgeon All-Stars last year."

"I have a number one on my shirt, which means I was the starter last year and I will be again this year," said the other goalkeeper, as the rest of the dressing room fell silent. "It doesn't matter that you played for Sturgeon whatever. Your dad used to play pro in Europe. You got this tryout because Daddy begged Coach Muller."

Branko's eyes narrowed. "I am good enough. You'll see." *But*, he thought to himself, *did Dad call Coach Muller?*

The other goalkeeper turned, picked up a water bottle, and lobbed it over to Branko. Branko stepped aside and allowed the full bottle to hit the floor with a thud. Water slowly seeped onto the concrete, creating a puddle by the door.

"Why'd you do that?" asked Branko.

"Why?" said the other keeper. "So you get used to your job. You'll be carrying my water bottles. Carrying my stuff."

That's how it's going to be, sighed Branko. He went to the other end of the dressing room, opened his bag, and began to change into his soccer gear.

No one spoke to Branko after that. He and three other keepers, including the one who insulted him, walked out of the dressing room, onto the green turf, and towards a net set up at the far end of the gym.

Coach Muller waved over the four goalies.

"Boys, boys, over here," he said, putting his arm around the bottle-thrower. "Good to see you, Brian. I trust you've been playing a bit this winter? Ready to play this season?"

"I'll play as much as you need me to," replied Brian, staring at Branko.

"I'm ready to play, too," said Branko. But he felt like he needed to go to the bathroom. And he also wanted to throw up.

"I have seen Brian play," said Coach Muller. "As for the rest of you, this is your chance to impress me. Now, let's get to work."

Brian, Branko, and the two other keepers laid down on the turf as Coach Muller and three assistants dropped balls towards their stomachs. Each time a ball was dropped, the goalkeeper would sit up, catch it, throw it back to the coach, and then lie back down. After a few of these drills, their stomach muscles burned.

"Another!" barked Coach Muller. "Another!"

After Coach Muller gave them a five-minute water break, Brian nudged Branko and pointed to the sideline. "What's going on? Isn't that your dad?"

Branko's eyes followed the direction of Brian's pointing hand. Yes, it was his dad on the sideline, talking to a bearded man in a green Selects t-shirt.

"Yeah. And?" Branko said, clenching his fist. The only thing keeping him from using that fist on Brian was the knowledge that if he punched a teammate, he'd be banned from the Selects for life.

"What's he doing talking to my dad!" screeched Brian.

That was Brian's dad?

Branko's voice went very quiet. "I have no idea."

After the break, Coach Muller asked each goalie to take a turn in net while the other kids took shots. Brian went in first and parried away a series of shots.

"Branko, you're up," said Coach Muller, as Brian strode confidently away from the goal.

But Branko wasn't paying attention. He was too busy watching his dad and Brian's dad chatting on the sideline. *What could they be talking about?*

"Branko!" Coach Muller yelled.

Branko's head snapped around and he saw the coach shaking his head. Branko dashed off towards the net. As soon as he got to the goal line, Coach Muller blew his whistle. Then, a shot came. Branko palmed it away. A lofted ball came in, and Branko caught it. But he could feel Brian's eyes on him. Branko had been making easy saves like this for years, but he couldn't get the butterflies out of his stomach. Another lob came, and the ball bounced around in Branko's hands before he managed to get a firm grip on it.

"If that had been a game, the other team would have scored," Brian yelled.

More shots came. Branko saved most of them, but each time one went in, even if it was a rocket of a shot that went off the post and bounced across the goal line, the young keeper felt his heart skip a beat.

Would Brian have stopped that? Should I have stopped that?

After the two other keepers had their turns, Coach Muller blew the whistle and told the boys to start doing their cool-down exercises. Branko started jogging around the field. One of the keepers was called over to see Coach Muller. The coach shook the boy's hand and gave him a reassuring pat on the head.

He'd cut one of the boys less than two hours into the new season!

Coach Muller then called the other three keepers over.

"Boys, we have three keepers left and two jobs up for grabs. I'll make my decision after practice next week. Be here on Saturday at eight a.m."

After practice, Branko emerged from the dressing room to find his father on the turf, still chatting with Brian's dad. Brian stood nearby, red-faced. "Branko." Josip pointed to Brian's dad. "This is Mr. MacLachlan. I haven't seen him in years. Brian was maybe four years old when we last met."

Branko put out his hand for Mr. MacLachlan to shake. "So, did you meet my dad on the Edmonton semipro team?"

"Dad, can we just go?" Brian interrupted.

"Brian!" scolded Mr. MacLachlan. "No, Branko. I used to be a supervisor at the grain terminal in Edmonton. Your dad used to work there, too, when he first came to Canada with Marta. After a few years, your dad got promoted and left to run the elevator in Morinville."

"Frank and his wife used to help your mom and me with our English," said Josip. "Brian, good luck this year."

Branko and his father left the complex and got into the truck. Branko turned to Josip as soon as the doors were closed.

"Dad, why did we pick this team? They already have a goalie who played here last year, and I might not even make the team!"

"I know this team has a goalie," replied Josip. "*Every* team has a goalie. Just because he was here last year doesn't mean he has the job, guaranteed. And if you start off as the backup, practise hard. Show the coach why you should be number one. We used to have a saying at my old soccer club — in practice, you earn your job, and in games, you *keep* your job. You can't just have the top spot handed to you. Not when you're a kid. Not when you're an adult."

"But Mill Woods said if I went there, I could start."

"Sure they did. Mill Woods will get nowhere near provincials. Ever. The Selects are one of best teams in the province. I would rather have you come here and learn from Coach Muller. And you will get along with Brian. For the team's sake. Not just because his dad is an old friend."

Branko stared out the window. He'd been so excited to get the chance to play for the Selects, and now he was dreading the drive into Edmonton next weekend.

"Or maybe you're not very serious about playing."

"No, I am. I want to be . . . be . . ."

"Be what, son?"

"Just like you, Dad."

"No, you don't," replied Josip as he turned the key in the ignition. "You want to be *better* than me."

21

3 NEIGHBOURHOOD BULLY

Branko burst through the doors of G.H. Primeau School and pulled his jacket tight to his body. A white blanket of snow settled on the soccer field behind the school, a soccer field that Branko had not, at any time in his life, seen anyone actually play soccer on.

Scottie, wearing a blue and orange Oilers jacket — and a blue Oilers toque — was waiting on the sidewalk.

"There you are!" said Scottie. "I've been dying to know how the tryout went yesterday."

"Not great," said Branko. "I think I can make the team, but, if I do, I'll probably be the backup. And the guy who was the starting goalie last year hates me."

"If you make the team, I'll put it in my blog."

"Don't bother. Being the backup isn't news," said Branko, kicking his boot through a soft pile of snow. "I won't be playing; I'll just be carrying the ball bag. And my life is going to be miserable with this other goalie who acts like he's playing in the pros."

"It's still a big deal if you make the best Tier-1 team in the province."

"I didn't say it was the best. I said it might be the best."

"Didn't you tell me they had a shot at winning the championship this year?"

"Yeah, but so do the Calgary Shamrocks. They make it to provincials every year."

"Branko, you were so excited to get that invite to try out. Now, it's like you don't care. For someone who loves soccer as much as you do, you have a hard time *talking* about soccer."

"I'm just worried I won't get to play."

"Well, it's a lot better to be the backup goalie for the Oilers than start for a team in the minor leagues."

"Scottie, did you just compare being a soccer goalie to being a *hockey* goalie?"

"Sorry . . . I keep forgetting how touchy you can be about hockey."

Even though the skies were already darkening, Branko could see figures on the sidewalk in front of the high school ahead. Ronnie Pelletier was standing with a group of older kids who had surrounded a younger student. Branko watched them take off the kid's hat and fill it with snow. They stuffed snow down the back of his jacket, then patted it down.

"Snow job. They get away with it because Ronnie's a star," said Branko. "No one will say anything about him."

Their victim slipped away and ran off down the sidewalk. Ronnie didn't chase the smaller kid — his attention had turned to Branko and Scottie.

"Hey there, reporter man!" he yelled, beckoning Scottie and Branko over. "Nice job. Nice job." Ronnie walked forward and slapped Scottie on the back. "Because of that, no snow job for you and your tall, gangly friend."

There were groans from Ronnie's entourage.

"I know, I know." Ronnie put up his hands. "I have decided to be merciful. And, trust me, it's mercy." He pointed at Scottie. "Have you ever seen this poor kid play hockey? He skates like this" — Ronnie ran in place — "and he falls like this" — Ronnie threw himself into the snow bank next to the sidewalk. "Look at me, I pulled a Scottie!"

Scottie's ears turned red as the group laughed.

But it was Branko who spoke up. "Come on, Ronnie — Scottie puts your name in the paper every week. He doesn't deserve that."

"No," Ronnie shook his head. "I put my own name in the paper every week. He writes the story, but I *make* the stories."

"Well," said Scottie, his voice shrill, "soon I will be writing about Branko! He's going to be the best goalie in the city! He's going to make the province's top rep team!"

"No way," said one of Ronnie's friends. "He's too skinny."

"That's because he's not a *real* goalie," said Ronnie. "He's a soccer player."

Now it was Branko whose ears burned.

"What a sissy sport," said Ronnie. "I think I score more goals in a day than a soccer team scores all season!"

"Are we done?" said Branko, starting to walk away. His path was blocked by Ronnie's friends.

Ronnie was about to answer, but he was interrupted by a yell from up the sidewalk. It was Ronnie's twin brother, Rejean.

Oh no, Branko thought. *Now it's gonna be both of them.*

"Ronnie!" yelled Rejean. "One of these days someone is going to say something, and coach is going to suspend you."

"Hey, I'm just having fun," cried Ronnie.

"Sure, fun, fine. But we've got too much on the line to pick on junior-high kids." Rejean looked at Scottie. "Hey. I saw the story in the paper today — thanks. Now, go on home."

Branko shoved his fists in his jacket pockets as they walked away, and a crumpled, soda-stained piece of paper fell out. Scottie leaned down and plucked the piece of paper out of the snow. It was a newspaper clipping with a picture of three soccer players hugging each other. Their team had just scored. A crowd in the background waved blue flags.

The article that went with the picture was written

0 1021 0233097 8

in another language. Something about . . . NK Osijek?

Branko snatched it from him. "My favourite team. Osijek. Grandpa sent this in the mail last week. He sends me all the match reports."

"He hasn't heard of the Internet?" said Scottie.

Branko pretended not to hear his friend. He looked at the picture, folded up the paper, and stuffed it back in his pocket. "You know, Osijek's goalie hasn't allowed a goal in four matches now. He's going to get a call to the national team."

"The Croatian team, right?" asked Scottie.

"Yes. Of course. What other teams are there?"

4 SPECIAL DELIVERY

When Branko got home from school, he found Josip sitting in the living room. There was a yellow parcel in front of him on the coffee table. "Another package from Djed?" Branko said.

Josip nodded as Branko ripped open the envelope. Inside was a collection of Croatian soccer magazines. Branko's grandfather, his *djed*, had, as usual, written notes in the margins. Some pointed to great photos. On other pages, the names of players were underlined.

Branko looked up at Josip. "Why does Djed do all this? Doesn't he know that we can watch some of the matches online and that we see all the match reports right away?"

"Humour him," said Josip. "It's his way of watching the games with us. He sees them, makes notes, and tells us what he thinks of the teams and the players. I like it, actually. So much more than a simple email that takes thirty seconds to write. Don't you?"

"I guess so." Branko picked up one of the magazines

and found a letter paper-clipped to it. It was written in Croat, but he could read the language well enough to understand it.

"Congratulations . . . your dad told me you were asked to try out for the top team in the province. Maybe one day you'll come back home and play for one of the clubs here, or even for the national team. We would be so proud!"

"He always mentions us coming home," said Branko.

"Home," sighed Josip. "What is that? Really? The place where I was born? Or back in Osijek, where I played? I'd argue that this place is home. Your mother and I came here to get away from a civil war. When the war began, home didn't feel like *home* anymore."

Branko could see the sadness in his father's eyes. "Dad —"

The telephone rang. Josip answered, then beckoned Branko over. "For you. It's Coach Muller." Branko's heart was in his throat. There was only one reason Coach Muller would be calling. *I am going to be cut!* thought Branko.

"Branko, you there?"

"Y-y-y-yes, Coach."

"Okay, I just need a second. I have news. You remember Stephen, the keeper who was trying out with you and Brian? Well, his parents just let me know he's going to go to Mill Woods instead. The team needs a keeper and he knows he will get all the playing time there. So there won't be another cut. You and Brian have made the team."

"Thanks, Coach." Branko swallowed nervously. "Have you . . . have you made your decision about who's going to start?"

"Yes. Brian was solid in net last year, so I'm making him our keeper. You have a lot of talent, Branko, but you looked shaky during the tryout. You still have some work to do. I'm looking forward to coaching you this season, and if you do well in practice, you could be the starting keeper next year."

Branko's stomach twisted itself into a knot. *A whole season with no playing time!* He and Coach Muller said their goodbyes and hung up.

"What did the coach want?" Josip asked.

"He told me I'm on the team," Branko said, then sighed. "Because one of the other keepers decided to go to Mill Woods. Not Brian, the other kid."

"Doesn't matter how you got it. You have the chance, now take it!"

"It's no chance at all. I'm the backup."

"That's fine. You'll learn a lot working with Coach Muller." Josip stood up. "You know, you haven't talked to Djed since before the tryouts started. Tomorrow morning, before you leave for school, you should call him to tell him the big news. First thing in the morning here is middle of the afternoon for him."

"Dad?" Branko said. "When do you think I'll

actually get to meet Djed face to face?"

"I've offered to fly him out here," Josip said. "But he always says 'no' for this reason or that. I think he's just set in his ways. It used to be very hard to leave the country under the old system."

"Couldn't we go to Croatia? I'd like to see the beaches and the sea. From the pictures you showed me."

"I don't know, Branko. It's hard for us to go back there. I'd need to take more time off work than they can spare, and . . . and . . ."

"And?"

"It's just too tough right now."

★★★

The next morning, Josip was in the kitchen, putting the breakfast dishes into the sink. The smell of last night's cabbage rolls was still strong in the kitchen. He washed his hands and moved to the hallway, putting on his weathered, blue winter coat.

"Branko, don't forget to call," he said as he left for work, walking out the door into the darkness. The sun wouldn't be up for another half an hour.

Branko still had some time, almost an hour, before he needed to begin his walk to school. He picked up the phone and punched in the numbers that were written on a pad next to the phone. Country code. City code. Then the local number. He heard the *buzz-buzz* of a European phone ringing half a world away. Then the click of someone picking up on the other end.

"Ya?"

"Djed, it's me, Branko."

"Oh, hello! Good to hear from you!" his grandfather said in Croat. "How are you? How did the tryout go?"

"Good news and bad news," Branko responded in Croat. "I made the team, but I'm only the backup goalie. Dad is happy, but I think it would have been better to go to another team where I could have been the starter. But Dad says it's better to be on the bench with the best than to be the best of the worst. Or something like that."

"He's right."

"But it's not easy." Branko sighed. *Not Djed, too.* "And the other goalie told me I got the tryout only because Dad used to play pro and he called the coach a bunch of times to ask him to invite me to play."

"Let me tell you something, Branko. You can't worry about how you got this chance. It's what you do with it that matters. You know what, Branko? Don't tell your father I told you this story, but, when he was fifteen, the local team didn't want to have him try out. Coach said the goalie position was filled with some kid from another town and they had promised the backup job to another kid whose dad knew someone in the Communist Party."

"So, what did you do?"

"We did what people did in those times. We bribed the coach."

"*What?*" Branko couldn't believe his ears.

"We had money and a few things that we could trade. And the coach could trade those things to get his boys some equipment. So, your father tried out. And they could see he was good, so they gave him the backup spot. Whenever they put him in net, he made great saves. Eventually, he earned the starting job and the out-of-town kid became the backup."

"What happened to the goalie they had originally promised the backup job to?"

"He was turned into a striker. He was terrible!" Djed sighed. "Look, Branko. I'm not proud of what we did. But in Yugoslavia in those days you had to bribe people to get *anything* — a plot of land, or the chance to buy a car. And I knew your father was good enough to show everyone he deserved to be the goalie.

"I don't know if your dad helped you get this chance or not. But in any case, you can't let it worry you. You will prove yourself. And when it happens ..." Djed paused. "I would love to see you come back home. To play here. To start a great career."

"That would be amazing!" Branko paused. "But could I do it? I was born in Canada."

"Oh, yes. Since your parents were born here, you are allowed to play for the national team. And you don't want to play for Canada, do you? When does

Canada ever make the World Cup?"

"I would love to play in Croatia one day. But for now, I just wish I could come visit you. I asked Dad again if we could go. He went on about how we don't have time. I think we do have time. We could make time. I don't get it."

"Sometimes, Branko, it's harder to go home than to visit a stranger. You know, the last time your father was in Croatia, he was with your mother. This is where they met and fell in love. I think your father doesn't want to come back here because it will remind him too much of Marta."

"But what about me? I'd like to see Croatia."

"Look, enough. When your dad is ready to come home, he'll come home and bring you with him. Okay? By the way, did you get the magazines?"

"Yes . . ."

"There's a good story about Osijek's new goalie. A guy named Saric. He got his shot after the starter got the flu and couldn't play. The first game, Saric didn't allow a goal. The next game, Saric didn't allow a goal. Now he's the number-one goalie. And he probably doesn't feel bad at all about how he got his shot."

5 FLUKE GOAL

The rain had been soft and steady; it was the kind of cold spring rain that made you wish it was snowing instead. Branko sat on the bench, enduring the icy downpour. He'd put on his jacket and drawn the hood the second he'd left his dad's truck, but he was still soaking wet underneath his rain gear.

I should have stayed in bed, Branko thought. For the first time since he had played Atom soccer, he was starting a game on the bench. When he'd played with Sturgeon County the previous season, he hadn't missed a minute of action. And even though he had known for weeks that Brian was going to start, he felt embarrassed sitting there by the ball bag. He felt like the handful of parents who had bothered to brave the rain to watch the match were all staring at him.

An hour before, the Selects players had arrived at the Edmonton Soccer Centre thinking that the referee would tell them the game against Three Lions was off.

But they were scheduled to play on one of the

artificial-turf fields. And the ref said that, unlike the grass fields that made up the rest of the complex, the fake stuff was holding up well.

So, Branko took some shots in warm-up, did his stretches — and took his place on the bench. His father sat in the stands.

Three Lions wasn't expected to be very good. The team had finished dead last in the Under-14 league the previous season. But Coach Muller had warned his team not to be cocky. "They can beat anyone in this league," he had told the players in the sideline huddle just before kickoff.

The first half of the game did not go well. The ball splashed through the water that had accumulated on the turf. And, with the cold weather and the fake grass, no one wanted to come in with a hard tackle. By halftime, neither team had put a shot on goal. Coach Muller called his players together.

"Boys, you have to move the ball a lot faster," he said. "These guys haven't come close to our goal yet. So, defenders, move up. Join the attack. Let's press these guys."

As the huddle broke, Branko looked towards the stands to see how his father was holding up. His eyes went wide. Sitting next to his dad was a boy in a blue rain slicker. In his right hand was a camera. In his left hand was an umbrella, which he was using to keep the rain from falling on the camera.

Scottie!

Branko stood up and furiously waved his arm, signalling that Scottie should come to the sideline. Scottie nodded, hopped off the bleachers, and trudged over.

"What are you doing here?" Branko hissed.

"It's your first game with the Selects. I got a ride into Edmonton with my dad. He dropped me off here on the way to the mall."

"I didn't tell you about the game today! I told you I didn't want a story! Why are you snooping on me?"

"Really, Branko? *Snooping*? Your team has something called an 'official website.' And on that website is a schedule and these words: 'Support the Selects. Fans welcome.'"

"So, you're going to write a blog about me sitting on the bench?"

"No, I was planning to write a blog about your first appearance as a member of the best Under-14 team in Alberta. Even on the bench, that's pretty darn good."

★★★

Two minutes into the second half, the Selects left back made a deep run out of his defensive position into the Three Lions' side of half. He made a decent pass to the centre of the penalty area, where the Selects centre forward was able to control it. But, as he turned to shoot, the forward slipped on the wet turf and the ball rolled harmlessly to the Three Lions goalkeeper. The keeper rolled the ball out quickly to a teammate, who then played a long ball. The ball landed in the spot where the Selects defender should have been. But he had left his defensive area to come forward. Branko could hear the *pssh-pssh-pssh* of the defender's feet on the wet turf as he dashed to get back in position.

It was hopeless. A Three Lions forward got the ball and dashed towards the Selects' goal. His right foot swung through the ball. Luckily the shot came right towards Brian. He put his hands up to catch the ball.

But the wet ball skipped right through Brian's gloves.

"No!" screamed Branko from the bench.

The ball dropped behind Brian and rolled across the goal line . . . 1–0 for Three Lions.

"What was he doing?" Branko yelled towards Coach Muller. "It's raining! He can't take that chance! He has to punch the ball away, not try to catch it!"

Coach Muller turned and glared at Branko. He didn't need to tell his backup keeper to be quiet. The look was enough.

The goal, though, shook the Selects out of their doldrums. Within two minutes, they tied the game, as their striker got his head on the ball from a corner kick and directed it into the goal.

Three Lions pushed their forwards back, just focusing on defence, trying to preserve the tie. But the Selects' quick fullback made a daring run up the field and got free when his marker fell down on the wet turf.

He moved into open space and, as another defender charged him, he pushed the ball forward for the striker, who let go a vicious shot that found the top corner.

The final whistle blew. Branko and the other subs who hadn't played got up off the bench and shook hands with their teammates as they returned from the field.

Brian met Branko. Water rolled down the starting keeper's face. He was shaking.

"Cold?" Branko asked.

"Yeah," Brian replied.

With that, the conversation was over. Branko turned away and there was Scottie, holding the camera, pointing it at Branko's face.

"What?" said Branko. "Scottie, please put that thing away."

"Look, Branko, I'm going to post video clips on the blog. Why not say something?"

"We won. I'm cold. Enough?"

"But —"

"Scottie . . . enough! Write what you want."

★★★

Branko and his father sat in the cab of the truck. They moved down the dirt road that led from the soccer centre out onto the street.

"Not a very good game," Branko said.

"Shush, Branko. A win is good. You know how

people call soccer 'The Beautiful Game'? Well, the person who came up with that saying is dumb. Yes, sometimes it's beautiful. But sometimes you win ugly. A lot of the time, actually. You know what they call a team that wins games like that twenty times a year? Champions, that's what!"

Branko bit his lip. He tried to hold back. But he couldn't.

"Dad, I know I'm better than him. I should be in net."

"Shush! Respect your teammate!"

"Dad, he saw one shot the whole game! And allowed one goal? What happens when we play somebody good?"

"Whoa, whoa, Branko. The important thing today is not you. Not Brian. It's the win. I saw you jump up and down when Brian gave up the goal. Not good, son."

"But . . ."

"But what, Branko? Do you know how proud I was to be the number-three goalie at Osijek? I didn't mind that I had to carry the water bottles for a bit. I was part of the team! And, you know how I got to be number two? I waited for my chance. And number one? I waited for my chance!"

"But Dad, you *got* that chance."

"Yes! And you know why? Our top goalie got signed by Red Star, the best team in the country. Until then, I worked *with* him, not against him! And you know what happened to him when he got there? Backup! He was happy to be the backup on the best team!"

"He was the backup because he was a Croat. They signed the best Croat keeper and then put him on the Serb team so he couldn't play anymore."

Josip hit the brakes on his truck. It stopped dead on the muddy dirt road that led out of the soccer centre.

"Son," Josip said, quiet, looking forward into the rain. "You put that away. Now. Your mother and I left the country so we could get away from all of that. We knew we wanted a family and we didn't want our children to have that hate. You will never, I mean, *never*, say anything about a Serb or a Slovene or a Bosnian ever again. I know you must get some of it from the magazines Djed sends. Maybe we shouldn't have taught you the language."

"Sorry, Dad, I didn't mean ..."

"No, son. I am sorry ... Sorry for so many."

6 SHOWDOWN IN THE GYM

Josip pulled back the heavy gym door, just a crack. Just enough to peek inside. His son, wearing padded goalkeeper's pants and a Croatia World Cup 1998 replica jersey, waited next to him.

A small, hard orange ball fizzed towards a net at one end of the gym. Boys with plastic sticks whacked away at it. It was then fired towards the net at the other end of the gym.

Branko took a turn looking through the crack. "They aren't leaving, Dad."

"It's not seven yet. They have till seven." Josip looked up at the clock in the school hallway.

"Have you finished your stretches?"

"Yes, I'm ready to go as soon as we get in."

On the outside of the gym door was a sheet that read "STIMAC, 7 P.M." next to the day's date. On a line underneath was "FLOOR HOCKEY, 6 P.M."

Josip tapped a finger on the spot where their name was and looked up at the second hand on the clock again.

Five. Four. Three. Two. One.

Josip pushed the door open wide and whistled as loud as he could. "Okay, boys. Time's up."

One of the boys stepped forward. It was Ronnie Pelletier.

"C'mon . . . it's a tie. We'll be done soon."

"Look, boys, it's done. Our name is on for seven o'clock. Time to pack up."

Josip didn't wait to hear Ronnie's protest. He walked to a wall and pulled away a mat that was leaning up against it. He laid it on the floor. Then, another.

Ronnie turned around and retrieved the orange ball. He flicked it with his stick over to his brother.

"Play."

"What?" said Rejean.

"Play," said Ronnie, a little louder. "Game on."

Rejean flipped the ball in the air with his stick. It didn't hit the floor. Josip caught it in his right hand. He placed it in the pocket of his Osijek jacket and went back to the task of laying down mats.

"Oh, come on!" cried Ronnie. "You're going to stop our game so one person can have the gym to himself?"

"No, I'm stopping the game because our name is on the schedule," said Josip.

Ronnie's eyes turned to Branko. He glared at the soccer player.

"Dad," Branko said, his eyes still locked with Ronnie's. "Wait. Maybe we could let them finish their game."

"Look, if they want to stay, they can stay and watch," Josip said, smoothing another mat on the floor. "But it's your time to put in the work."

Ronnie allowed his eyes to leave Branko. Then a wicked smile crossed his lips. "You know what, that's a good idea!" He waved to the other floor-hockey players. "Move the nets aside. We're going to stay and watch."

"Dad!" Branko squealed.

"No, it's fine," Josip said to his son. "It's good to practice in front of an audience. It puts more pressure on you. Helps you learn to focus."

The boys moved the hockey nets and then all of them sat down in a row against a wall.

"All yours," said Ronnie.

"The mats are ready," said Josip, motioning his son to go stand on them. He turned to the hockey players. "We're going to do some drills. Branko will stand on the mats while I shoot. Branko must stop the shot, get up, stop the next shot."

Branko sighed and opened the ball bag he had brought into the gym.

As soon as the balls had rolled out of the bag, Josip pounced on them. He put one ball under his left foot, rolled it to his right, and . . .

Thunk!

The ball crashed off the gym wall behind Branko and bounced wildly on the floor.

Crack!

Another ball off the wall.

Ronnie called out, "You suck, Branko!"

"What? We've started? I couldn't get to either of those!" Branko yelled.

"Oh, so you are going to ask the other teams you play to tell you when they are going to shoot?" called Josip. "Maybe they should tell you if they are going to shoot right or left, just to help you out?"

The hockey players laughed.

"A good keeper is always ready." Josip had another ball at his feet, ready to shoot. "Look at how you're standing. On your heels. How can you move to get the ball when you're on your heels?"

Josip fired another ball. Branko reached out an arm, but the ball deflected off it and smacked off the wall behind him.

"Goal," his father said. "There was no force in your punch. You need to move your arm through the ball — don't just stick it out."

"But . . ."

"But what, son? We have been doing this for, what, a minute?" Josip pointed to the clock on the wall of the gym. "A game is ninety minutes. Look, I don't want to force you to do this. If you want, we can just let these hockey players have the gym back."

The group sitting against the wall cheered.

"Dad, you *know* I want to do this."

"Show me footwork, then."

The shots came. High. Low. Branko lifted himself onto the balls of his feet. How the arches in his feet burned!

Another ball came at him, dipping slightly. His dad had hit it off the knuckles in his foot so the ball wouldn't fly straight. Branko bounced two steps to his left and drove his arms outward. The ball hit his hands and went sideways. Branko crashed down onto one of the mats. His side was sore from diving; the mats only slightly softened the blow of hitting the hard gym floor.

"Better," Josip said. "And you didn't leave the ball in front for a rebound. Good. Push the ball away from the goal if you can't catch it."

Branko got up quickly. He knew his dad was going to shoot as soon as he was on his feet.

More shots. At his feet. At his chest. Low to his right. High to his left. Branko felt like his ribs were on fire as he stretched to deflect a shot. Each time a ball bounced on the floor, it made a popping sound. When it hit the wall, a cracking sound. *ThudthudthudCRACK!*

And what was that sound?

Branko was so focused on the balls coming at him that he almost didn't notice the new sound. Almost.

It was applause. Someone was clapping.

"Rejean, what are you doing?" Ronnie glared at his twin brother.

"C'mon, Branko . . . you're doing great!" Rejean called out as he clapped.

Branko dove to his right. Pain exploded in his elbows and knees. He got his hand to the ball. He was up just in time to dive in the other direction.

"That's it!" cried Rejean. "Stick with it!"

One by one, the other hockey players started clapping with Rejean. With each save came a roar. Soon, all of them — except for Ronnie — were cheering every time he made a stop.

Rejean looked at his brother. Stared at him hard. Ronnie didn't look up. Instead, he got up and walked out of the gym.

Josip stopped, pick up a ball, and walked towards his son.

"Lay on the mat."

Branko sighed. It was going to get worse.

"Faster, Branko," yelled Josip.

Branko laid down on the mat. He felt the pain in his shoulders as they hit the blue padding. His dad hovered over him, ball in his hands.

"Now!" Josip said, throwing the ball down at Branko. His son rose up to catch the ball and tossed it back in the same motion. It was like doing a sit-up while catching and throwing the ball. Josip tossed the ball back. Another sit-up.

"Come on, son!" Josip yelled. "Move. Move!"

Finally, the ball slipped out of Branko's hands and hit the floor.

Rejean groaned.

"Enough. We are done," said Josip.

"Did I do okay?" asked Branko.

"Okay. Not great. Okay. You still have a long way to go. You must be tough to play for a full ninety minutes. It's when you get tired that you start making mistakes. You must learn to fight through it."

Josip turned and walked away. Branko got up off the mat. He noticed a dull pain in his right arm. He rolled up his sleeve and saw a deep, blue bruise on his forearm.

He felt a hand on his shoulder. It was Rejean.

"Look, Branko," Rejean rolled up his pant leg. There was a scar across the back of his calf. "Skate caught me here last season."

"Looks painful."

"It was. But you keep going. Got to. Can't let my brother make it to the NHL without me!"

Branko looked up and saw the other hockey players pulling up and folding the mats. "Don't worry," Rejean said. "I asked them to help clean up. You've worked hard enough."

"Hey . . . thanks, Rejean. That's really nice of you."

Rejean's focus was somewhere else. "Your dad is tough. He reminds me a bit of my dad. He built Ronnie and me a backyard rink, then set up a net with targets on it. He'd keep us out on the ice until we hit all the targets."

"But you made your dad proud in the end," Branko sighed. "You guys are the kings of this town. I don't know what I need to do. I work my tail off. I joined a team that doesn't give me any playing time because my dad said that was the best team for me to be with. I do all the things that he wants, and he just walks out of the gym like all I do is disappoint him."

"Hey, my dad is the same. He's not going to be happy until we've each got a Stanley Cup ring. Maybe not even then."

"Wow," Branko sighed, and scooped the balls into the bag. "Well, thanks again for putting away the mats, Rejean. I'll see you around." He slung his bag over his shoulder and walked out of the gym, down the hallway and then into the parking lot. His dad was sitting in the truck.

"So?" Josip said as Branko gingerly stepped into the cab. "Tomorrow, we'll work on penalty kicks."

7 BRANKO'S CHANCE

The Selects were off to a perfect start to the season: undefeated in their first three games. Since the game against Three Lions, Brian hadn't allowed a goal. Branko, though, didn't quite share the team's joy. Oh, he forced some smiles and high-fived his teammates when they came to the bench. But, deep down, Branko wanted the Selects to lose. If Brian allowed another bad goal or two, Branko might get his chance.

But, the match against Mill Woods didn't offer Branko much hope. Brian made a good save early in the game, leaping to punch away a bending free kick the opposing forward had smacked towards the goal. Then, the Selects struck right before the halftime whistle. The Selects striker leaped high for a corner kick, and the ball looped off his forehead and into the corner of the Mill Woods' goal.

At halftime, Brian sat down on the bench next to Branko. Neither keeper said a word to each other.

A few minutes into the second half, Mill Woods got

a chance to tie the game. A long shot on goal deflected off a Selects defender and the ball went across the end line. The Mill Woods players massed in the box, hoping to get to the ball after the corner kick.

Brian jumped to beat a Mill Woods striker to the lofted ball. The striker slipped and fell into Brian as he was in the air. Brian flipped over and landed on his outstretched right arm. There was a cracking sound as he hit the turf, which was hard as a rock after a couple of weeks without rain.

Players on both teams cleared their benches. Frank MacLachlan, Brian's dad, hopped out of the stands and ran onto the field. Coach Muller was already pushing his way inside the group of players to attend to the boy who was laying on the ground inside the circle.

Branko could hear Brian's cries. He got up and started to cross the touch line, moving to join his teammates around Brian. He was stopped by a hand on his shoulder. It was Josip. "Come on," Josip said, then went to the ball bag. He pulled a ball out and tossed it towards Branko. "You must begin warming up."

"But, Dad, Brian's hurt over there!"

"Yes, I know. His dad is there. Coach Muller is there. Frank already called an ambulance. There's nothing else we can do. But you have to be ready to play. That is how you help your team."

Branko didn't move. His eyes were fixated on the field. It just felt wrong to be on the sidelines while the rest of his teammates and his coach were trying to help a teammate who was in obvious pain. He felt guilty that he had been wishing Brian was out of the game. For months, he had been dreaming about getting the chance to be the Selects' starting keeper. And now the chance was staring him right in the face, and it didn't feel right.

"Look, Branko, you must put it out of your mind," said Josip. "Don't think about it. It is sad, yes, but part of the game. Now you must start getting ready!"

Josip dropped the ball to his feet and kicked it towards Branko. His son reached down and picked it up. He held onto it, as if he was cradling a baby.

Josip grabbed another ball and placed it on the ground. This time, he didn't kick it gently. He followed through mightily with his right foot, and the ball crashed into his son's shin.

"Get ready!" Josip growled.

Branko nodded and began running in place. He did some jumping jacks, all while keeping his eyes on the field. Frank had propped Brian up into a sitting position. Branko's stomach turned as he saw Brian's right arm, limp and crooked, by his side.

"Probably a compound fracture," said Josip. "Son, keep warming up. Don't look."

They heard a siren in the distance. Then, they saw dust churning up off the dirt road that led into the soccer centre. The red lights of the ambulance could be seen through the dust cloud. The ambulance lurched onto the field, coming to a stop right next to the Selects' goal.

Two paramedics got out and went to Brian.

"He'll need surgery if it's a compound fracture," said Josip.

"Dad! Can you please stop talking about the injury!" cried Branko, as he jogged in place on the sideline.

The paramedics strapped Brian to a stretcher and wheeled him into the ambulance. Frank dashed to the parking lot, started his car, and drove off so he could meet the paramedics and his son at the hospital.

The referee cleared the field. "All right, coaches! Take five minutes to gather your teams."

Coach Muller ran towards Branko. "Don't worry, Brian is going to be okay. I know it's tough to see someone get hurt. But you have to get ready. We have the lead and there's about thirty minutes left to play. Just ride out this game and then . . . well . . ."

"Yeah," said Branko, swallowing. "I know. I'm the guy now."

Coach Muller leaned over and whispered in Branko's ear. "I know it's not easy. But this is your team now. You can't worry how you got this chance. You just have to make the most of it."

Branko squinted his eyes and looked at his coach. "Excuse me. Have you ever spoken to my grandfather?"

★★★

The pickup sped north on the highway that led back to Morinville. Branko sat next to his father with the cell phone to his ear.

"Yeah, so then Coach Muller sent us back out to finish the game. I could tell he was nervous. He made another substitution, so we'd have five defenders instead of four. He wanted to make sure that Mill Woods didn't get a shot on me. Because of Brian's injury, the ref had to shorten the game to seventy minutes, because two more teams were waiting to play."

"And, did they get a shot?" asked Scottie. Branko could hear chatter of the crowd at the Morinville hockey arena in the background. Scottie had to yell into the phone.

"It looked like the coach's plan would work . . ."

"Wait!" Scottie yelled more forcefully. "Sorry, I can't hear you. You need to speak up."

"It looked like it was going to work," Branko spoke as loudly as he felt he could without making his dad drive off the road. "But, right before the end, they got one chance. They got a free kick outside the box. I called for four men in the wall, but the shot came around them. But I dove and I was able to stop it."

"And you won?"

"Yes!"

Branko heard a massive roar over the phone.

"That could be the goal that does it," said Scottie. "Ronnie from Rejean. This place is jumping!"

"What's the score?" Branko asked.

"That makes it 3–1 for Morinville. I don't think there's any way back for North Edmonton. This win gets us into provincials!"

Branko was quiet, just listening to the roar of the crowd. The Selects might have had twenty people out to their game — and they were all parents. He imagined what it would feel like to play for a full house; what it would feel like to make a great play and hear the crowd go wild.

"Look, Branko. I'll put a little something on the site about your debut. I will. It's just that the Warriors are close to provincials and the whole town wants the paper and the website to follow their every move. But once the Warriors finish their season, I'll be back to watch your games."

8 GREAT DAY FOR A PARADE

"Branko, I'm surprised at you," Josip said as he walked into the living room. "You're always saying you don't understand hockey and wondering why everyone else likes it so much. But here you are — absolutely riveted by a hockey game."

"I'm not riveted," said Branko. "There's nothing else on TV."

"Okay," Josip shrugged. "Whatever you say."

It was a wonderful Alberta spring afternoon. The sun was beating down brilliantly and there was just a hint of a chill in the breeze. But Branko had no urge to be outside. He stared at the screen, watching Ronnie Pelletier skate up the ice.

"If they win, the mayor said she'll throw a big party for them on Sunday," said Josip. "Your game isn't until the evening, so you could go to the parade in the afternoon."

"Dad. They haven't won yet. In fact, no one has scored yet."

"I can't believe they put a kids' game like that on the television."

"Dad, it's not just a kids' game. It's the Bantam provincial final. There's been so much hype about the Pelletiers being the best prospects since Gretzky that the sports channel decided to pick up the game. And . . ." Branko was distracted by the action on the screen. Ronnie whistled a shot just wide of the Cochrane goal, then slammed his stick on the ice.

Cochrane's defenceman picked up the puck and fired it forward. It hit the centre who had just jumped off the bench on a line change. The puck stuck to the centre's stick as if the black tape on the blade was Velcro.

The centre dashed in towards the Morinville goalie. The goalie came out to challenge the shooter, but the centre shifted the puck to his backhand and went around the sprawling netminder. All he had to do was slide the puck home — but the puck slid off his stick and softly kissed the post. The goalie, scrambling to get back in net, was able to smother it.

Branko pumped his fist in the air.

"I saw that," smiled his father as he sat down. "I thought you always cheered *against* Morinville."

"I . . . um . . . am," said Branko, his cheeks turning red. "I'm just frustrated, can't you see?"

Josip laughed. "Frustrated. Okay."

But, through two periods of the game, the two most frustrated people in Alberta were the Pelletier brothers. Cochrane kept them off the scoreboard. Every time they jumped on the ice, they were poked, prodded, and grabbed.

The third period was different. Rejean Pelletier wiggled his way out of the clutches of a defenceman, then retrieved the puck deep in the Cochrane end, spun around, and fired a cross-ice pass for his brother to tap in.

"That's what we've been waiting to see!" cried the play-by-play commentator.

On their next shift, the Pelletiers struck again. Rejean found Ronnie with a breakaway pass that he slid through the legs of two opposition players. Ronnie went in alone on the goal and used the exact same move the Cochrane forward had tried the previous period; Ronnie took the puck on his backhand, went around the goalie, and — unlike the unlucky Cochrane centre — slid it across the line.

Ronnie got his hat trick a few minutes later when his brother sent him a perfect pass from behind the net.

The camera followed the Warriors as they mobbed each other at the final whistle. Branko heard a car horn honking in the distance. There were whoops coming from the neighbours' houses.

Josip applauded. "That Rejean kid, he is very good. Very special."

"You mean Rejean and Ronnie. Ronnie scored all the goals."

"No, I meant Rejean. His brother may have scored all the goals, but Rejean *made* the goals. He's the one who reads the game and sets up all the plays."

"Dad, I thought you hated hockey."

"You watch it and it's really not that different from soccer," said Josip. "The team that is better at passing, wins. The team that hustles, wins. And never once in my life have I said I disliked hockey. You're the one who hates hockey. Or *did* hate hockey, I think. Sort of like you used to hate those Pelletier brothers."

"Rejean's all right. I'm happy that he won the provincial title. But the thought of Ronnie winning something makes me sick. He's just such a jerk."

"Well, think about what I said," said Josip. "I have always found that players who aren't confident are the ones who talk the most. There's always one guy on every team who's tough to get along with. We had a striker at Osijek who scored on the first day of the season and he wouldn't shut up about it for a month. All he did was talk about that goal — but it was the only goal he ever scored for us. Coach cut him about two months later."

★★★

The next day, the population of Morinville swelled. Usually, seven thousand people called the town home — but this afternoon was different.

Vans from the TV networks were parked in the courtyard of St. Jean Baptiste Church. Sports networks, national news broadcasters, and newspaper reporters all huddled together in the park. At the edge of the park, where it opened onto Morinville's main street, hundreds of people perched themselves on the curb, waiting for the parade of pickup trucks to go by.

The parking lot of the supermarket, right at the corner of Morinville's one and only traffic light, had been cleared of cars. Instead, it was filled with hockey fans. Not just people from town, but folks who had driven in from Edmonton and even from Saskatoon — six hours away.

"This is all for the Pelletiers," said Scottie to Branko. They balanced themselves on the curb, in front of a crush of fans pushing forward. "It's not about the whole team. It's about them. That's why the people are all here. They want to get a glimpse of these guys before they go off to junior and, one day, the NHL. It's like the chance to see Gretzky when he was a kid."

"Did Ronnie tell you that yesterday?" laughed Branko. He was already wearing his Edmonton Selects tracksuit. Underneath it was his uniform. He had his gloves and cleats in a pack that was slung over his shoulder. He'd watch a part of the parade, and then meet his dad at the end of the main street, where it wasn't closed to traffic, and they'd begin the drive to Edmonton for his game.

"No, Ronnie didn't talk to me or my dad yesterday," said Scottie. "He talked to the TV people and then he just left. Rejean was the one who talked to us."

"I betcha Ronnie will talk a lot today," laughed Branko.

A local chapter of the scouts walked down the street in their brown uniforms. Then came some riders from the local horse club. Their white horses spun in circles on the street.

The mayor came riding by in an old convertible; she sat in the back, so the crowds could see her easily. She tossed candy out to the curbs for the children to retrieve.

Then came two Mounties, dressed in red serge uniforms and black knee-boots. Their brown, wide-brimmed hats protected their faces from the bright sun beating down from the sky. Each Mountie had an arm in an ear of the provincial championship trophy. The crowd roared as it went by. Television cameramen dashed onto the street to get close-up shots.

Then came four pickup trucks. In each of the first three that went by there were seven players standing in the bed, wearing their Warriors jerseys. They waved to the crowd and received warm applause in return.

But the final truck, a cherry-red pickup, had only two passengers in the back — the Pelletier brothers. Ronnie and Rejean waved to the crowd. Ronnie blew a kiss as the cameramen drew near to the truck.

For a moment, Branko had felt like he could join the crowd and cheer for the Warriors. But when he'd seen Ronnie blowing kisses and waving his arms in the air, the feeling had disappeared.

"I need to go soon," he yelled to Scottie, trying to be heard over the crowd. "Have to get ready for my game."

"Branko, your game isn't for hours," Scottie yelled back. "You have plenty of time. But I admire your work ethic. That's why you're gonna get one of these parades down the road."

"That's a joke. Selects could win provincials and I could play a whole season without giving up a goal — and no one would notice."

9 A COSTLY GOAL

Branko stared down at the grass. Maybe, just maybe, a hole would magically appear. He could leap down and plummet into a cavern. That would be far better than having to face Coach Muller and his teammates when the final whistle sounded. As if it wasn't bad enough to have had to watch Ronnie Pelletier get a roaring ovation from the entire town of Morinville earlier that afternoon, now this had to happen.

The Selects were preparing to kick off, but Branko didn't want to look up.

For the last minute, he'd been replaying the sequence in his head. An easy cross had come in from the right wing. With the score at 0–0, the West Edmonton Athletics had been happy with trying to escape a game with a draw against the first-place Selects. Their coach had ordered the team to kick the ball deep into the Selects' half, then pull back and get ready to defend in numbers.

So all Branko had to do was make an easy catch.

The kind of catch a goalie will make a dozen times in an average game.

Staring the grass, Branko could see the play in his mind as if he was watching it on TV. He saw himself reach up, then saw the ball squirt through his gloves. He looked back, helpless, as the ball slowly bounced over the goal line.

A shrill sound interrupted Branko's thoughts, followed by a roar from the West Edmonton bench. The final whistle. The Selects had lost their first game of the season.

Branko slowly walked towards the sideline. He was the last man on the field to make it back. None of his teammates spoke to him.

Slowly, the Selects pulled off their cleats, rolled down their socks, and put their shin guards in their bags. Still, no one made eye contact with Branko. No one spoke. Brian sat on the bench, his track jacket slung over his right shoulder. Underneath, his arm was in a sling. He didn't look in Branko's direction, even though he had no shoes or socks to occupy him.

"Hey!" Coach Muller yelled. "Everyone, freeze!"

Great, Branko thought. *Coach Muller is going to call me out in front of the whole team.*

"Okay, I've been watching how every one of you reacted when that goal went in! And now not one of you has spoken to your keeper! Not one word of encouragement! Okay, guys, I get it. Mistakes happen.

But pick up your teammate!"

Coach Muller turned around to walk away. Branko felt everyone's eyes turning to him.

Then, Coach Muller spun another time. He had more to say.

"And, if you want to blame the goalie for this loss, may I remind you that we didn't score a goal! That's on the whole team. You can't win without scoring a goal, right? Am I right?"

Coach Muller left. The boys around Branko slapped his back and said, "Don't worry about it" and "We'll win the next one." But Branko still felt terrible. He knew his teammates were only speaking to him because Coach Muller had told them to — and that actually felt worse than not having them talk to him at all. And Brian didn't say anything — he just stared straight ahead. He had a little smile on his face that seemed to say, *I know I wouldn't have let in such a soft goal.*

After the boys changed their footwear, Branko walked over to his dad, who put his arm around his son's shoulder.

"These things happen," said Josip. "Even the greatest goalies ever have made mistakes. The sign of a great goalie is how he bounces back. You have to move on."

Frank MacLachlan intercepted them in the parking lot. Brian was next to him, his track jacket draped over his bad arm.

"So, Joe, we good for next week?"

"Yes," replied Josip with a friendly wave. "It'll be good to get together with the boys."

As they got in the cab of the truck, Branko turned to his dad.

"What's this about next week?"

"Canada's got their World Cup qualifier next week in Toronto. I thought it would be nice to have the MacLachlans over to watch the game on TV."

"What? Dad! That means I have to spend the day with . . . Brian? He *hates* me. And we're going to watch Canada? That team has no hope of getting close to the World Cup! Doesn't Croatia have a qualifier that day? I thought we were going to watch that . . ."

"The Croatia game is first thing in the morning," said Josip, putting his key in the ignition. "We'll watch that over breakfast and the Canada game in the afternoon. Time zones."

Branko groaned. Next Saturday would be a long day.

"Don't groan," said Josip. "Frank and the family were always good to us. It'll be good to get back together."

"Back together? I don't know these people!"

"But you did. You were just a toddler. Before your mom . . . well . . . you know."

"The cancer."

"Yes. We'd spend a lot of time together. And, when

65

your mom died, you were so young. And I — well — just lost contact with a lot of our friends. I had to focus on you and on work. Getting you to school, to practices. Helping you grow up. Between the job and that, friends moved into the background."

"Dad, we had time. We could have gone over for dinners or hung out."

Josip looked hard at his son. "Yes, I guess we did. But that was our life before your mom was gone. So, even when I'd see Frank at work, I'd think about Marta. I remembered how good life was before the cancer. And, well, maybe I didn't want to be reminded of that. Maybe it was too tough, son. For me."

The pickup truck moved out of the parking lot. Branko closed his eyes and tried to remember his mom. There were flashes, like dusty old photographs. He had to think hard to remember what she looked like before she got sick. By his third birthday party, she was already thin. Nurses came to the house to check on her. Her skin was waxy, yellow.

Branko looked forward at the road. All of a sudden, losing that game didn't seem like such a big deal anymore.

10 CANADA OR CROATIA?

Rap! Rap! Josip got up from the living-room couch and opened the door. Frank, his wife, Maggie, and Brian stood outside. Brian had a black-and-white Selects jacket draped over his shoulders. The cast on his right arm and the accompanying sling made it impossible for him to use one of the sleeves.

"Come in, come in!" Josip smiled.

On the living-room table were cookies, set out on a fine-china serving plate. There was also a silver coffee pot and small china plates with blue floral patterns that Branko had never seen before.

"Dad," Branko had said that morning as he watched Josip polish the silverware. "I didn't even know we had this stuff."

"We have guests," Josip had responded. "First time in a long time."

Now Maggie walked into the house ahead of Brian and Frank. She gave Josip a hug. "So good to see you, Joe," she laughed. "It's been too long."

Josip offered seats to all three. "We have a few minutes before the game," he said. "Please, have some coffee."

Brian scooped four cookies onto a plate and sat next to Branko. "One of the benefits of being injured — I don't have to be on a soccer player's diet. So, what do you think about today's game? Canada has the home-field advantage. I don't know much about the El Salvador team."

"Uh, hi, Brian," Branko said. That was all he could squeeze out of his mouth. Brian had just said more to him in twenty seconds than he had over the past two months — and he seemed friendly. "I think Canada can win, sure."

Branko looked to his father.

"Um, Dad, can I go to the other room?" asked Branko.

"Yes, you can," said Josip. "Why don't you go show Brian your room?"

Branko sighed. He didn't want to. But he knew it was important to his dad that he try to be nice to Brian.

"You can show Brian all your soccer stuff," said Josip.

Brian followed Branko up a short flight of stairs and down a hallway.

"C'mon in," Branko said as he opened the door. Brian's eyes went wide when he entered the room. Branko's room didn't have any posters of action heroes, movie stars, or video games. A blue scarf, with OSIJEK printed on it, hung over the bed. The bookshelf was filled with old soccer magazines in a language Brian didn't recognize. On the wall over the bookshelf was a large poster of a soccer team; the goalie in green, the rest in red-and-white checked shirts. The faces were faded, almost totally white. The ends of the poster were torn.

"And that is . . ."

"Our greatest team," said Branko. "Croatia, 1998. We finished third at the World Cup. Third! We were so close to winning it all. Some of the greatest players we've ever produced were on that team." Branko's finger traced the faces of the players on the poster. "My dad put this up in my room when I was just a baby. And it's been here ever since."

"Branko, I notice that you say 'we' a lot," said Brian. "Shouldn't it be 'they'?"

Branko went quiet for a second. He took a deep breath. "Actually, *we* won our World Cup qualifier today. I watched it on pay-per-view with Dad this morning. We beat Slovakia 3–1. Now we'll see how Canada does. I guess it'd be nice to see them win."

"C'mon boys!" Josip called up the stairs. "The game is about to kick off!"

★★★

The flat-screen television showed the images of a half-full stadium in Toronto. The commentators were talking about how Canada needed to win this game if it was to have a shot at making the World Cup.

Branko sat with Brian on the worn brown sofa, while the adults sat on fold-out chairs that were placed throughout the room.

Josip clicked the remote to turn the volume up a bit more.

The El Salvadoran national anthem played. A roar erupted from the crowd as they heard the trumpet flourishes. The camera showed the visiting team, each player's arm extended in a salute towards their flag.

When the anthem finished, a great cheer came up from the crowd. The broadcast showed image after image of blue-shirted fans waving blue-and-white flags.

"This would never happen in Croatia," muttered Josip. "You'd never see a game in Zagreb where more people were cheering for the visiting team than the home team."

Brian sat up a little straighter, wiggling around on the sofa because he could use only his left arm to prop himself up. He looked at Branko, then at Josip. "Okay, if Croatia was playing Canada, and we all went and bought tickets, who would you cheer for? Huh?"

"Brian!" scolded Frank.

Neither Josip or Branko answered.

Brian didn't let up. "Dad, I was in Branko's room. And he has a Hall of Fame in there for Croatia, not Canada. There's not one picture of a Canadian player on his wall!" He turned towards Branko. "C'mon,

Branko. One day you might get the chance to play for Canada. But what if someone in Croatia called and said 'Come over and play for us'?"

What a tough question! Branko knew that Djed would be so proud if he'd come back and stride onto the grass at the national stadium in Zagreb. He'd play in front of tens of thousands of fans waving red-and-white scarves printed in the famous Croatian checkerboard pattern. And Canada? To make the team and have nobody recognize you on the street?

Branko found an out. "Look, Brian, making a national team, *any* national team . . . not going to happen."

"Why not, Branko?" said Brian. "You're the best goalie in this league."

"What?" said Branko. *Why is Brian complimenting me?*

Canada kicked off the game and there were whistles and catcalls from the stands. The Canadians flashed forward in their all-red uniforms. The commentators talked about the starting lineup and the soccer clubs each Canadian normally played for. Enrique Salas, Canada's midfielder, played for FC Edmonton. Most of the others played in Europe. The goalie played in Denmark, while the left winger had just signed to play in the Japanese League.

"And they all make the long flights back just to be booed at home," sighed Frank.

"See Salas there?" said Brian. "I've gone down to see him play for the Eddies. He's from Edmonton. He played for Mill Woods when he was a kid. He was born in Chile, but he grew up here. He chose us over Chile. He plays for Canada."

El Salvador's nifty central midfielder fired a shot from the top of the box at the Canadian keeper. It bounced awkwardly on the grass and skipped over the keeper's outstretched hand.

The cameras showed a section of blue-shirted fans jumping up and down, then moved back to the player celebrating the goal. He fell to his knees and blew kisses to the crowd.

Down a goal, the Canadian team pushed towards El Salvador's net. Enrique Salas got the ball up to the top of the box, brought his left foot down, and sent the ball flying into the roof of the net, just under the bar.

In the den of the Stimac house, there was applause, and a loud "Yeahhhhhhhh!" from Brian.

Salas dashed the length of the field towards the south end of the stadium, where he could celebrate the goal with the small but dedicated throng of Canadian supporters who had gathered there. A fan in the front section dangled a Canadian flag over the railing separating the stands from the field. Salas grabbed it and kissed the Maple Leaf.

As the game crept towards halftime, with the teams locked in a 1–1 draw, Branko told Frank and his dad that he wanted to get some more snacks from the kitchen.

"Brian, can you give me a hand?"

"Well, my good hand," Brian replied.

They walked into the kitchen and Branko turned to Brian.

"Okay, I need to ask you something. You've hated me all season long, and now you're pretending to like me? I assume you're just doing this so you won't get in trouble with your dad."

Brian sighed. "Look, when I heard we were gonna hang out, I was probably as mad about it as you were. And, yes, my dad had a talk with me. He asked me why I didn't like you. You showed up at tryouts and I hated your guts. And my dad asked me why."

"Okay, why?"

"Because I didn't want to lose my spot to some new guy. I would have hated *any* hotshot keeper that Coach invited in. And then I did get the starting job, but I broke my arm. That wasn't your fault. But, for some reason, I wanted to see you fail. That game when you gave up that last-second goal, I wanted you to stew over it. So I didn't say anything."

"You let in a bad goal, too."

"Sure, and you let me stew over it. Look, we weren't being very good teammates. My dad said so. Coach Muller said so."

"My dad says so, too."

"Look, I'm down for the rest of this season. I was angry at first — I was disappointed. But I want to help the team. And that means I want to help you."

73

"Okay," Branko said. "It would be good to have a teammate to talk to."

"That's right — because no other player will talk to us goalies!" laughed Brian. "Look, I'm not always gonna be nice to you. I'm gonna tell you when you mess up. I'm gonna tell you when I think you're slacking. But, I know some of the players in our league from last season. I can tell you about their moves."

"Deal!" Branko reached out his hand, then felt awfully dumb. How could Brian shake hands with his right arm in a sling?

But Brian just kept laughing.

11 THE SUPER SAVE

"This footage is *amazing!* I can't wait to put this online."

Scottie sat in the backseat of the cab of Josip's truck, playing and replaying scenes from the soccer game on his digital camera.

Branko, sitting in the front seat next to his dad, turned to look back at his friend. "I guess I got lucky."

"Call it what you want," said Scottie. "But I call it a great story. In fact, I might just run these two clips on their own on the newspaper website. I might not need to write anything to go with them."

The Selects had been playing at home at the Edmonton Soccer Centre, on a lush field in the corner of the complex. Instead of sitting in the stands, Scottie had chosen to shoot Branko in action from behind the goal during the second half of the match. Because of that decision, the footage was clear, crisp. Branko looked big in the picture when he dove to his left.

"So, Branko, what was running through your head when you saved the penalty kick?"

"Are you interviewing me?" Branko squealed. "Here? In the truck?"

"May as well. We have a half-hour drive," Josip said.

"Yes, I need some quotes," Scottie said as he reached into his pocket and pulled out a curled-up notebook and a pen that had been chewed at one end. "First off, that's the team's eighth win in a row. You have given up just two goals over those games. What's your secret?"

Branko looked forward. "Practice," he answered.

Scottie sighed. "Look, Branko, you are going to have to work on this. When a reporter asks a question, try to do more than a one-word answer. Smile. Have fun."

"Okay," Branko nodded. "Practice and . . . and . . . well, I have fun practising. And preparing."

Scottie shook his head. "So, again, what were you thinking when the penalty kick was taken?"

"Which one?"

Josip snickered at his son's answer. "Now you sound cocky."

"The second one," Scottie said.

Branko thought back to the shot. It was as if it had happened in slow motion. The Selects were up 1–0 on St. Albert. But Dean Thiessen, St. Albert's star striker, had placed the ball on the penalty spot and was waiting for the referee's whistle so he could run up and put his left foot through the ball.

Branko had guessed Thiessen wasn't about to repeat the same mistake he'd made in his first penalty kick.

The first time, Thiessen had stared at Branko like he was trying to burn a hole through the goalie with his eyes. His shoulders were rigid, square. Before Thiessen took a step towards the ball, Branko already knew that he had picked his spot — right down the middle. It was just like Brian had told him during the halftime break: *Thiessen doesn't always pick corners.*

Thiessen had been sure Branko was going to dive to either his right or his left when the ball was struck, that the ball would just go down the middle and in, right through the spot where the goalkeeper used to be.

So, Branko had stayed rooted to the ground, and the ball had caught him in the chest. Thiessen had given himself away with his body language.

But the second penalty attempt had been different. Thiessen hadn't looked up. He hadn't given Branko the chance to look into his eyes.

One step towards the ball; a second step. Branko saw the left foot come through the ball. Branko guessed left, diving towards the post.

It was a good guess. The ball headed to his left, but fast. Thiessen had got all of it. Branko stretched out his arm as far as it could go. When the ball hit his fingertips, the goalkeeping gloves did little to stop the pain. Branko felt the nail on his middle finger rip away.

Then, he heard the thud of the ball off the post.

As he came to a crashing halt in a cloud of dust, Branko watched the ball pop off the post and start to float in the air. The ball flew over his head, shoulders, and torso.

But it was as if his foot had a mind of its own. Branko lifted his right leg. The ball deflected off the back of his heel and away from goal. Even though he was down on his belly, he wasn't beaten.

Branko had stopped the ball twice on the same shot.

"Branko? Branko?"

"Sorry, Scottie," Branko shook his head vigorously, pulling himself back into the present. "I was thinking about the play."

"You dove just as he shot. Lucky guess?"

"Yes."

"No," Josip interrupted. "Not totally a guess. What do you call it in English? An 'educated guess.' Stopping a penalty isn't just diving right or left. It's a game. Like chess. Branko saw the first shot go right down the middle. He knew the shooter wouldn't go back that way again. So, he looked for the tip-off . . ."

"Dad!"

"Yes, son?"

Branko shook his head. "We shouldn't give away all the secrets."

"Okay, okay. Scottie, don't print this. I have something to say to Branko. It's not enough to just read the play. You can also control it. Make the shooter think he is guessing. Distract him. You are in trouble if he puts the ball down on the spot, runs through, and kicks it.

That means he's feeling confident. You want him to be worried. Get him to look up at you. Make him look you in the eye. Make him look at the net. Make him second-guess himself."

"How? It's a big net," interrupted Scottie.

"Big to you. When a guy is taking a penalty shot, it looks smaller and smaller by the second. If he looks at the net, he will feel the pressure. He will think about missing. And once you have him thinking about missing, he will miss."

"Scottie, can you play me back that second penalty kick?" Branko asked.

Scottie handed his camera to Branko. Branko didn't watch himself; instead, he kept his eyes on Thiessen. After he hit the shot, the St. Albert striker turned around and slid, raising his arms into the air to celebrate.

He never saw Branko make the save. As the Selects defender kicked the rebound out of play, the camera closed in on Thiessen, who was now running towards his bench, jumping after every third or fourth step.

The referee frantically tried to chase Thiessen down. Finally, the official caught his quarry by the sidelines. The ref pointed back towards the net. Thiessen fell to his knees, his hands on his head.

How embarrassing!

Branko looked up from the camera and tried not to laugh. He pursed his lips together.

Hard.

12 INTERNET SENSATION

"Is that Djed on the phone? Is everything all right?"

Branko had heard his father break into Croat after he'd said hello. That was a worrying sign. Often, when they got a phone call from Croatia, it was bad news. Maybe a relative had died or had lost a job.

But then Josip laughed. Hard. So much that he dropped the cordless phone on the floor. He picked it up and apologized, and motioned for Branko to come over.

"It's Djed, all right," said Josip. "Here."

Branko said hello to his grandfather. He was greeted with an excited stream of words. Because Branko didn't hear Croat very often, he had a hard time keeping up if someone was speaking fast. And, boy, was Djed excited. Something about "goalkeeping" and "star"?

Josip took back the phone and said his goodbyes. He hung up the phone.

"What was that about?" asked Branko.

"Well, how often do you think your grandfather uses the Internet?"

"Djed?" scowled Branko. "I don't think Djed has *heard* of the Internet."

"Well, your Aunt Magda took him to an Internet café today. Seems like your cousin was on the Internet and saw you. He spread the word through the family. And Djed went with Magda to go see it."

"Saw me?"

"Scottie's clips from the St. Albert game, I think. Djed said it was the best save he'd ever seen a keeper make. Better than anything I'd done at Osijek."

"Okay; let me get this straight. You're telling me Djed *discovered* the Internet today — and then he saw me?"

"Yes. Look, you need to get your bag ready. We have to leave for the game."

★★★

Scottie climbed into the cab of the truck and slid into the backseat, placing his backpack down next to him.

"I hope I can file a story to the website after today's game," he said.

"Why's that?" asked Josip.

"Because the site is down. My dad had to bring in some tech guy to look at it. We set some kind of crazy record today with the traffic."

"What?" asked Branko. "Why would so many people want to see the Morinville paper?"

"Duhhhh," said Scottie. "You."

"Me?"

"Yes, that save. Everyone wants to see it."

"But that happened last week," said Branko. "Why would it crash the site now?"

"Well, someone posted the link on Facebook or Twitter or something and then the video went viral. And we can't handle hundreds of thousands of hits."

"Branko's grandfather saw it in Croatia earlier today," Josip said. "Amazing how fast it goes."

"That's the thing. Once one person posts the link, then ten more post it," said Scottie. "Then ten more. And there are no borders."

"But it's not like I did it playing for Arsenal, or even for FC Edmonton!" said Branko, scratching his head.

"Doesn't matter," said Scottie. "People are writing 'best save ever' when they go on Twitter or Facebook or whatever other site. So people click on it. They don't care if it's in a big stadium or a school gym."

The truck rolled into the long dirt driveway that led to the Edmonton Soccer Centre's parking lot. It was full. Cars were parked in the aisles and along the fringes of the lot.

Josip grumbled. He put the truck in reverse and found a spot along the side of the entrance road.

"Looks like a bit of a longer walk for us today," said Josip as he hopped down from the cab and then opened the rear door so Scottie could step out.

Josip and the two boys walked down the dirt road,

through the parking lot, and towards Field No. 1, which was right next to the changing rooms and the cafeteria in the middle of the complex.

But this walk to the field was much different than any Branko had experienced this season. The bleachers on the far side of the field were full. Fans ringed the field. As Josip and Scottie looked for a decent spot from which to watch the game, Branko had to lower his shoulder and push through the crowd so he could get to the Selects' bench.

"There he is! The goalie!"

"You sure?"

"That's him!"

Branko heard the voices as he made his way towards his teammates. He felt the eyes on him. He even heard some rounds of applause.

Brian sat on the bench as some of the Selects were pulling on their socks and cleats.

"Hey, rock star," said Brian, as Branko sat his bag down on the bench.

"Hey."

"It's funny," Brian said. "We're in first place, we've scored the most goals in the league, and everyone is here to watch our goalie. Figures. And they're gonna be disappointed. You probably won't have anything to do tonight."

The Selects were set to play the last-place team in the Under-14 Tier-1 division. The South Side Eagles hadn't won all season long. And they hadn't scored much, either.

At the half-hour mark, as Branko stood in the goal, he heard boos. The Selects were already up 3–0, and Branko had touched the ball only twice, both on goal kicks. Each time the Eagles made a bad pass or kicked a ball out of bounds, there were groans.

Finally, late in the first half — after the Selects had scored two more goals of their own — an Eagles striker pushed behind the back line and barrelled towards Branko's goal with the ball at his feet. Branko heard the crowd begin to clap.

The striker got to within ten yards of the goal line and drove his foot through the ball. He leaned back as his foot met the ball, and it went over the net. The crowd groaned.

The ball was tossed back towards the field, and Branko put his foot through it — a mighty goal kick that soared to the halfway mark of the field. The crowd broke into applause.

They're clapping louder for the goal kick than for any of our team's goals, thought Branko.

13 SHOWDOWN IN ST. ALBERT

The 8–0 win over South Side put the Selects within just one point of winning the Edmonton area's Tier-1 title, which would earn the team a shot to go down to Calgary for the provincial championships. But they'd need to get that point against St. Albert, whose only loss this season had come to the Selects, thanks to Branko's two penalty saves.

The game was in St. Albert, a small city located between Morinville and Edmonton. Just as they'd found at the Edmonton Soccer Centre, the parking lot was full. Josip backed the truck out onto the street and parked about half a block away from the entrance to the soccer complex.

Scottie hopped down from the cab before Josip and Branko made it out. He saw a large crowd milling about in front of the complex.

Branko made a path through the masses. His eyes were riveted on the Selects' bench. Or, more accurately, on the person who was standing next to the Selects' bench.

It was Rejean Pelletier, wearing a Brandon Wheat Kings jacket. He'd been selected by that junior hockey team in the bantam draft and would be heading to Manitoba in a couple of weeks. The Wheat Kings had made a blockbuster trade to ensure that they could draft his brother, too.

Rejean shook Branko's hand. "You soccer goalies aren't as weird as the hockey goalies, are you?"

"What do you mean?" Branko shook his head. "I don't think I'm all that weird."

"Hockey goalies are freaky. Don't talk to anyone. Sit in the corner of the dressing room by themselves," Rejean slapped Branko on the back. "No, seriously. Good luck. You are doing the town proud."

"I'm sure no one in Morinville knows I'm here."

"Oh, you'd be surprised. Your name is in the paper a lot, now. Anyways, I'm going to go sit in the stands over there and fight off the autograph-seekers."

Branko sat down next to Brian on the bench.

"You know a Pelletier?" Brian gawked. "Cool! Which one is he?"

"Rejean, the nice one," Branko said as he looked down into his bag, pulled out his shin guards and socks. He didn't look up as he shook off his training shoes and started putting on his gear. "Okay, let's go over what we talked about on the phone."

"Right," said Brian. "Ciaran O'Hallaran. He didn't play the last time we faced St. Albert. He's replacing

Thiessen in the starting lineup. I know a guy on the St. Albert team; he told me the coach was choked that Thiessen ran and celebrated like he'd scored on you when he should have followed his shot and looked for a rebound. O'Hallaran just got back from an injury, and the coach made the switch. I played against O'Hallaran last year. Best striker in the league. He'll be on Team Alberta with you when you get called to nationals."

"No one's called me about Team Alberta." Each year, an elite coach took the best Under-14 players in the province to make up an all-star team that would go to the national championships.

"They will."

Branko shook his head.

"Anyways," Brian continued. "O'Hallaran is sneaky. He has a way of getting open in the box. And he likes to shuffle before he shoots. Instead of shooting, he'll move a bit to try and change the angle."

"Thanks, Brian."

"Seriously, this shuffle thing is important. Last year, he beat me. He dropped his shoulder like he was going to shoot. I went down to block the shot, but the shot didn't come. He raised his shoulder and took two more strides. I was helpless. He put the ball in the open net. He made me look stupid. He's never played you, so he'll think you don't know a thing about him."

St. Albert was so worried about the Selects' attack that it began the game concentrating solely on defence.

When the Selects got the ball, every St. Albert player retreated into their own half, crowding the field. With so many men back, St. Albert made it nearly impossible for the Selects' offensive players to complete passes. "Don't push up too much!" Coach Muller shouted at his players. "They need to attack sooner or later! They want us to over-commit on offence, then come at us with a counterattack!"

Maybe it was the roar of the crowd that prevented the Selects from hearing the coach's words. Or maybe the boys were just too focused on scoring goals on a team that was playing like it didn't want to fight back. But the defenders pushed up too far. The midfield lost its shape. And, when the Selects lost the ball in the St. Albert end, they didn't have enough defenders back when the home team surged forward. O'Hallaran led a charge of three St. Albert players against just one defender.

Coach Muller threw his clipboard down onto the ground.

But the crowd *oohed* and *aahed* in anticipation. They were finally going to see the YouTube sensation, Branko Stimac, in action! O'Hallaran sent the ball wide left to his winger, then dashed towards the box. Branko knew the cross was going to come back into the middle. He bravely came off his line. O'Hallaran threw himself forward to make contact with the ball that had been lofted towards the penalty area.

Branko charged out, eyes on the ball. He heard

O'Hallaran's feet pounding, louder, louder. He was coming right for him! Branko threw up his arms. Even though he knew he was going to collide with the St. Albert striker, he couldn't take his eyes off the ball.

Reach, reach, reach, thought Branko. *Catch.*

Branko's hands grasped the ball, then he felt pain in his ribs. The breath was knocked out of his lungs. The grass came up fast into his face, then the grit of dirt in his mouth. Still he held the ball. He heard the referee's whistle. The crowd's roar turned into stunned silence.

Branko felt the weight of O'Hallaran on top of him. He wriggled out from under the striker and rose up, ready to put the ball back into play. But the referee waved his arms. O'Hallaran hadn't risen from the ground.

Branko rolled the ball away, out of bounds, the gentlemanly thing a player does when someone is hurt on the field. Branko knelt down. O'Hallaran moaned, and there were dribbles of blood coming from his mouth. He opened it to yell in pain, and Branko saw the wide hole where two front teeth should have been.

St. Albert's coach and someone who Branko guessed was O'Hallaran's dad — they had the same curly red hair — helped the striker to his feet. But the coach turned to the ref and said, "We'll play with only ten men for now. He's gonna be okay."

"But it's a head injury," said the referee.

"No, he got hit in the mouth," said the man with the red hair. "My boy will be back."

"I'll be fffine," Ciaran said, spitting blood. "Ifff jufft the mouffff that hurffts."

Since St. Albert would be down a player until O'Hallaran was ready to play, the team pulled back into its defensive shell. And the strategy worked. With every St. Albert player in his own end, blocking shots and breaking up passes, the Selects couldn't create a decent scoring chance. And, learning from their earlier mistake, the Selects kept their own defensive players back, wary of a St. Albert break.

The teams went to halftime tied 0–0.

"We only need a tie to make it to provincials, but they need to beat us to make it," Brian said to Branko at halftime. "This 0–0 is no good for them. Sooner or later they're gonna have to come at us."

"I know, I know."

Rejean came down from his spot in the stands to visit the team. "That collision was awesome," he said, slapping Branko on the back. Branko winced.

Brian whispered in Branko's ear, "What is it? You hurt?"

"It's nothing," Branko whispered back. To Rejean, he said, "Glad you're enjoying the game."

"It's been all right," Rejean said as he started to walk back to the stands. "But tell your teammates I want to see some goals."

As the teams jogged back on the field for the second half, the crowd broke into applause — O'Hallaran was back. O'Hallaran smiled, showing a gaping black hole.

The return of their star striker gave St. Albert's players a boost; they moved to attack rather than defend. Branko was called upon to snag cross after cross; and O'Hallaran came charging into the penalty area as if he didn't remember the earlier collision with the Selects goalie.

As the Selects came down the right wing, Branko sensed there would be trouble. Instead of staying in the middle and waiting for the cross, O'Hallaran ran towards the sideline and took a short pass from his winger.

The Selects centre back tried to chase down O'Hallaran.

"No!" cried Branko, holding up his hand. "Stay in the middle! Stay in the middle!"

O'Hallaran stopped with the ball at his feet, waiting for the defender to come charging at him. Just as the defender began his slide, O'Hallaran toe-poked the ball off to the side and skipped over him. O'Hallaran caught up to the ball and turned towards goal. He lifted his left foot to shoot.

Branko could hear Brian's voice in his head. *Watch for the fake.*

The keeper remained on the balls of his feet; he fought the urge to slide out to block the shot. His every instinct told him to charge down the shot, but his brain told him to heed Brian's advice.

And O'Hallaran didn't follow through. Instead, he

pushed the ball ahead gently — and Branko was ready for him. As O'Hallaran shuffled, so did Branko. Finally, O'Hallaran put his foot through the ball, but Branko had the angle cut down. The shot hit Branko in the hands; he felt the sting through his gloves. O'Hallaran charged ahead to try to get his left foot on the rebound, but Branko pounced and covered the ball before the striker could get there.

The crowd roared. Branko looked up and saw Rejean in the crowd. The hockey star was on his feet, hooting and hollering.

St. Albert kept coming forward, searching for the goal that would break the 0–0 tie. But the save had boosted Branko's confidence. He dove left to stop shots. He tipped a headed attempt over the crossbar. He came running well away from his goal to collect loose balls.

The referee's assistant on the sideline held up a sign with the number three on it — a warning that the full ninety minutes had expired, and all that was left was three minutes of injury time. The referee checked his watch. The Selects held, knowing a 0–0 tie would be enough to win them the league and send them off to the provincial championships.

St. Albert threw players forward, desperate for a goal. The defenders joined the attack. The home team had no one even close to the centre line. All eleven players had come up, including the keeper.

Through the mass of bodies, Branko caught a

glimpse of a looping shot that was dipping towards the goal. Branko leaped and caught the ball, reaching over the crush of players.

Wait, thought Branko as he hit the ground. *They don't have a single man back.*

Branko rose quickly and hurled the ball down the field, where the Selects' fleet-footed striker was standing by himself. The striker got the ball on the Selects' side of half — which ensured he wouldn't be called offside. Then, all alone, he darted upfield, crossed half, dashed towards St. Albert's empty net, and scored.

The referee blew the whistle for full time. The Selects had won 1–0, scoring on their only shot of the second half. Branko ran to the middle of the field where his team had gathered to celebrate. Teammates jumped on his back, and he went crashing to the ground, hearing howls and laughter as he hit the grass.

But Branko felt pain screaming through his body as he went down. Grimacing, he rolled away from his teammates and staggered towards the sideline. Rejean and Scottie were there; Branko put his hands out in front of him, warning them not to touch him.

Scottie watched as Branko sat down and rolled up his shirt, revealing a series of deep bruises along his left side. Scottie could make out the outline of Branko's ribs — in blue.

"Wow," said Rejean. "You're hurt . . . bad."

14 NURSING AN INJURY

Branko laid on his living-room couch. Josip placed a plate of vegetables and sausages on the coffee table. The television was on; FC Edmonton was playing at home against the Minnesota Stars.

"We could have gone to the game, Dad," said Branko as he reached for the plate of food. "I'm feeling fine."

"No," said Josip. "The Selects don't have another goalie they can count on. You must rest. One more week and we go to Calgary for provincials. You have to be ready."

"Look, Dad," Branko said, pointing to his ribs. "I made it through the St. Albert game without a problem. They're just bruised."

"You made it through because of the adrenaline," said Josip. "Sometimes you don't realize how badly you're hurt until after the game. If the Selects had a game today, you couldn't play."

"Yes, I could."

"Well, you could put on a shirt, I guess," laughed

Josip. "You could stand in front of the goal. But the first time you had to dive or stretch, you'd be finished. So, for now, just sit and watch TV. We have a week to get you ready."

Branko knew his dad was right. It hurt if he took a deep breath. His ribs were sensitive to the touch. And when he lifted his shirt up, the left side of his abdomen was covered in purple-and-blue blotches. Deep down, he knew his dad had been right to give away their tickets for the FC Edmonton match to Frank and Brian.

It was the kind of day where the sun was bright and warm, but the air had a slight chill. Branko could feel the cool snap as the breeze blew through an open window, carrying the deep, musky smell of canola from the fields surrounding Morinville.

Josip sat down next to his son as Enrique Salas and his teammates got ready to kick off. He placed a package into his son's hands.

"You haven't opened this yet? It came yesterday."

"Sorry, Dad," Branko said as he cradled the package in his arms. "Just hadn't got to it yet."

"You must be thinking a lot about next week's game," said Josip. "Usually, you tear right into Djed's mail."

"Well, he's discovered the Internet now. He can just go to the Internet café and e-mail me. Or we could even Skype."

Josip sighed and then clapped his hands as FC

Edmonton came close to scoring. Salas had laid the ball off to the team's winger, who had then sent a scorching right-footed shot just over the bar.

"Look, son," Josip said. "It's a ritual. Djed sends these magazines because he imagines you, every week, waiting for them to arrive. He imagines you reading them over and over. It's his way of connecting with you. And the Internet isn't going to change that."

Branko nodded as Salas stole the ball and led another attack down the field, this time finding his striker, Marc Piette, with a pass that slid between the two Minnesota central defenders. But the linesman raised his flag; Piette was behind the defenders when the ball was played, and was called offside. The camera closed in on Salas, who ran over to Piette and tried to look him in the eye. Piette would not look back up at his teammate.

"He won't go offside next time," said Josip.

Branko put his fingernails under the tape that held the wrapping together and then began to tear open the package. He pulled the wrapping apart and three magazines fell out, along with a red-and-white checked scarf with the word HRVATSKA emblazoned in blue on it.

"Another national-team scarf," said Branko. "Well, school's going to start soon and I could use it. My old Croatia scarf is kind of ratty."

And there was an envelope, too.

Branko tore it open. Inside was a handwritten note, along with a creased picture of a goalie. The colours were faded as if it had been left out in the sun. The goalie was posing for the camera, pretending to be waiting for a shot. His hands were extended out in front of him, and he was in a shallow crouch.

It was Josip. How old was he in this shot? A teenager?

"This picture is you," read the note in Croatian. "This was your dad, but it is you. This was my favourite picture of your dad. He's young and he has so much hope, so much potential. Just like you.

"I can't wait to see you play. It made me proud to see you on the Internet. But you are so small on that screen and my eyesight is bad. I want to see you at a big stadium, waving to the crowd as you lead the team out of the tunnel.

"Your father was good. He was very good. Who knows what he would have done if the war hadn't happened?

"But, you know what? In his last letter to me, he told me something. That you're better than him. He didn't want me to tell you what he wrote to me. He thought it would make you cocky. But I think you need to know. Josip can be very hard-headed. He gets it from me. I never told him how proud I was of him. I always pushed him and said he wasn't good enough, that he could get better. And now he does that with you.

"But you make him so proud. He told me. And I

think that you should know."

Branko put down the letter and looked at his father, who was staring at the television. Salas slipped another ball through to Piette — and, this time, the striker wasn't offside. He took the ball and stroked a low shot that went off the left post and in. The camera panned to a small but vocal group of fans wearing blue FC Edmonton shirts and waving blue scarves.

15 PLAYING FOR KEEPS

"Look, you don't have to be a hero," said Coach Muller. "You can sit out."

Branko, Coach Muller, and Josip sat in the bed of Josip's pickup truck, which was parked in the Calgary soccer complex's lot. Josip had used a tent canvas to create a bright green canopy over the pickup bed. It was a good thing, too — it protected anyone who climbed onto the truck bed from the rain that had been falling steadily for the last forty-eight hours.

"Absolutely not," said Branko, looking into his coach's eyes. "I'm the guy. The backup we brought in hasn't played at this level all season. You can't just ask him to play in the final."

"Look, kickoff is two hours away," said Coach Muller. "I saw you in our morning workout. You could barely keep up a jogging pace."

"I'm a goalkeeper," said Branko. "You don't need me to run up and down the wing."

"Look, Branko. You've had a great year. You don't

have anything left to prove. You don't need to play. When you couldn't practice, I did as your father asked. I told the guys you'd caught a bad flu. I didn't tell them your ribs are bruised, that it hurts when you take a deep breath. And I stayed quiet two days ago. You got the start . . ."

"And we won," Branko interrupted. "And I didn't allow a goal."

"Yes, the semifinal went as well as I could have hoped, but I saw how you could barely get up after you made that diving save. Everyone heard you grunt or roar when you jumped to grab the corner kicks. It's no longer a secret that you're injured — at least to your teammates. Look, Branko. In the end, you're thirteen years old, and my job is to make sure you develop as a player . . . not to win at all costs."

"Wait, you mean you're going to pull me?" Branko squealed. "It's the provincial final! I have to play! Please!"

Coach Muller sighed. "Branko. In the end, it's not your choice. You're a minor. So an adult makes the call. If you were eighteen, you could decide whether or not you would play . . ."

Branko's heart sank. *Coach Muller is going to sit me out!*

"But it's not my choice either," continued Muller. "I'm your coach. I'm not your parent. The call on whether or not you play belongs to your father."

Josip took a deep breath. He put his hand on his

son's shoulder. "Coach, here are my instructions. If Branko shows any signs that he is struggling, you are to take him out. But, I know chances like this don't come along all the time. There will be important people watching this game. And then, there's the trophy. My son has worked hard for this. So, if he says he can play, and you are confident he can play, then he should play."

The coach nodded, then dragged himself out of the truck and walked in the rain towards the field where the championship game would be staged.

"Dad," Branko said. "Thank you."

"You know, son, sometimes your dad has to step in to make sure you get the chance. Let me tell you something — did you know that Djed gave some minor-sport ministry official about a year's worth of our savings so I could get a tryout with our local soccer team?"

"You knew about that?" Branko's eyes went wide. "I mean, Djed told me about that, but he made me promise never to say anything to you!"

Josip laughed. "Not to tell me? Oh my, I never brought it up because I didn't want to embarrass him! My very first practice, the coach started calling me The Bribe Boy. I was so ashamed. For about five minutes, that is. Then I began stopping the balls in practice. And the coach didn't call me Bribe Boy anymore."

"Dad, can I ask you a question?"

"Sure."

"Something's been bugging me all year. Was it you who got me the tryout with the Selects in the first place?"

"What do you mean?"

"Someone told me that I only got invited to tryouts because you asked Coach Muller to take me."

"Son, let me tell you this. I might have got my chance because Djed greased the wheels. But you earned this all on your own. Yes, I called. But Coach Muller told me he already had you on the invite list."

★★★

The game started off as well as the Selects could have hoped. Just seconds after the opening kickoff, the Selects right winger made a run with the ball at his feet and delivered a cross to the middle of the Shamrocks' penalty area. The striker jumped to head the ball. The ball glanced off his forehead and swerved towards the net, hitting the underside of the crossbar and then bouncing down past the goal line.

The game wasn't even a minute old, and the Selects had a 1–0 lead!

The Shamrocks pushed forward, hoping to tie the game. But Coach Muller moved the Selects' tough-tackling central midfielder to defence. Instead of the usual four defenders, the Selects were now playing with five, making a solid line in front of Branko's goal.

With no way through the back line, the Shamrocks

had to loft long passes over the defensive line, and then have the strikers try to chase them down. But when a ball went up and over the defenders, Branko came out of his goal and cleared it away, acting like a defender himself. Ball after ball came over the last defender back, and each time Branko was able to get to it before a Shamrocks striker.

The rain slashed down on the field, turning it into a quagmire. The field had already been soaked before the game, but the rain came down harder as the game progressed. Puddles of water could be seen on the grass. A small pond had appeared in front of Branko's goal. Branko was worried the game might be stopped by the referee — the rules stated that if a match was abandoned, the two teams had to start over again the next day. And, because the Selects were nursing a lead, each second was bringing Branko and his teammates closer to that big trophy. If they had to play tomorrow, they would lose their advantage.

In the stands, Josip, Scottie, and Scottie's dad huddled in their ponchos. Scottie tried to photograph the game through the driving rain. His viewfinder couldn't focus on the players because droplets kept obscuring the screen.

At halftime, Coach Muller gathered his players.

"Look, guys, the field is in bad shape. It's a terrible way for a provincial final to go. Just keep a solid line at the back. Sooner or later, they'll have to come at us in numbers to try to get that tying goal. Then, we can jump on them. And don't be afraid to shoot; in this bad weather, the ball can take a bad bounce on the grass — even what you think is an easy shot at their keeper is a tough one to save."

As the Selects ran out onto the field for the second half, the coach grabbed Branko.

"Are you okay?" he asked.

"Fine," whispered Branko. "All I have to do is kick those long passes out of danger. I haven't had that much to do."

"Keep an eye out," said the coach. "The Shamrocks didn't lose a game in Calgary this year. They are going to get a chance. And how are you feeling?"

"All right," Branko lied. Being out in the cold, miserable rain had made his ribs throb with pain. But he knew he couldn't show anyone that he was hurting. Not Coach Muller. Not the Shamrocks players. Not his own teammates. And not his dad.

The Shamrocks stopped trying to play long passes over the heads of the Selects defenders. Instead, they brought their defenders up into the attack and took long shots on net. The Selects kept their defenders back, but the Shamrocks kept pounding shots at them, hoping that sooner or later the ball would get through.

A shot deflected off a Selects player's thigh and looped towards the goal, but Branko was on his toes. He caught the flight of the ball, judged it well, and palmed it away from the net. As he reached up to deflect the ball, Branko felt the fire going up and down his side. He could feel his eyes tearing up from the pain, but he knew the rain would hide that.

As the game progressed, the Shamrocks brought more and more players forward. Their parents, huddled together in one stand, hollered and clapped, trying to rally their kids. The provincial soccer association had decided to erect extra temporary stands around the field because of all the attention Branko had attracted. But the rain had driven the fans back to their cars in the parking lot, where they tried to keep their eyes on the game from afar. Others had gathered under an awning in the covered patio of the soccer centre's snack bar. From there, they could see parts of the field through gaps in the temporary bleachers. Branko thought he had caught a glimpse of three men wearing FC Edmonton jackets huddled together. Were they looking at him?

As Coach Muller had predicted, the Selects got their break. The Shamrocks left winger slipped and fell as he came down the sideline. The ball was taken by the Selects fullback. He had no one in front of him and dashed up the sideline. Most of the Shamrocks players had come far forward and now had to scramble back as the Selects fullback ran into their end of the field.

The Selects striker streaked down the middle, following the ball carrier. The lone Shamrocks defender back had to make a decision: Should he stick in the middle to cover the striker, or should he run out to cut off the fullback at the sideline? He chose the latter option. He left the middle of the field and raced towards the sideline.

The Selects fullback didn't panic. He waited for the defender to get close, then chipped the ball over him. The ball came down in the middle of the field, near the top of the Shamrocks' penalty area. The Selects striker dashed in and dribbled the ball towards the goal, with only the keeper to beat. The goalie came out, and the striker gently poked the ball past him, then jumped over the keeper's sliding body. Now all he had to do was toe-poke the ball into the open goal. But he slipped on the grass as he swung his right foot through the ball; the slip caused his shot to go off line, and the ball hit the outside of the post and went out of play for a goal kick.

He had missed.

Branko jumped up in the air in frustration and let out a deep moan. *That should have been the insurance goal!* But, as he landed, he felt a surge of pain through his left side. He exhaled deeply, but that only made his ribs hurt more. He looked up the field, hoping that no one on either team would notice how he had grimaced in pain.

The Shamrocks came back at the Selects with renewed energy as the rain began to lighten. A long shot from the midfield crashed off a defender and went behind the Selects' goal line for a corner kick.

Branko got into position. He had a defender by

each post, standing on the goal line, ready to make a last-ditch clearance. Each Selects player called out the number of the Shamrocks player whom they planned to mark.

"You've got Seven!"

"I've got Five!"

"Look out for Eight at the top of the box!"

"Take Six short!"

The corner kick lofted the ball in the air. Branko decided his best course of action was to challenge for the ball. He could out-jump anyone on the Shamrocks and he could use his long arms to reach for the ball before it got to the head of any opposing player.

Branko got under the ball and jumped. But as he went up, he nudged a defender, who was backing in towards the goal line as he marked one of the Shamrocks strikers.

It wasn't a big collision between the players. In fact, the defender had just brushed Branko. But the contact had been directly on the series of bruises that lay underneath his jersey. Branko winced from the pain shooting from the left side of his rib cage to his brain. And he took his eye off the ball.

Instead of catching the ball, it bounced off his fingertips. The two sets of players scrambled to get to it first. A defender smashed at the loose ball — but it deflected off a Shamrocks player and came back towards the goal line. Branko, stunned by the pain, couldn't get there in time. The ball crossed the line, and then stopped in a puddle before hitting the mesh.

The parents of the Shamrocks players rose up from the stands, hooting and hollering.

Branko stared at the ball, sitting there, no more than a foot over the goal line.

My fault, he thought. *All my fault.*

Branko looked to the sideline and towards Coach Muller. The coach rolled his hands, one over the other — the hand signal for a substitution.

Branko caught the coach's eye and shook his head. *No way!*

But the coach put up his hands and gave Branko a thumbs-up. He wasn't making the signal so he could take out his keeper — he'd decided to bring in another forward. Instead of finishing the game with two strikers, he changed the formation so he could have three.

The switch almost paid off. The new striker had a big left-foot shot, and he used it from just outside the penalty area, but his attempt grazed the crossbar — and stayed out.

Branko put his hands over his face as the ball bounced away from the Shamrocks' goal.

The referee blew the whistle to signal the end of regulation time. Now, the teams would take a rest and then play thirty minutes of extra time.

Branko skulked towards the team huddle. The striker who had missed the open net pulled him aside.

"My fault," he said. "I should have gotten us that insurance goal. The net was wide open."

"No, my fault," said Branko. "I should have made that save. I had my hands on the ball."

"No, the rain is bad out there," said the striker. "You can't blame yourself. The ball's as slippery as a block of ice."

Brian pulled Branko aside and pointed over to the bleachers. "See the guy with the grey hair in the blue track suit, sitting under an umbrella next to those two other guys? That's FC Edmonton's coach!"

Branko cringed. The coach of Edmonton's pro team had just watched him let in a soft goal.

Coach Muller walked up to the boys. "We haven't lost yet. Don't feel sorry for yourselves. Back out there!"

Playing soccer on the muddy field was like playing in wet cement. After coming back from the break, the boys on both teams found it harder to run. Their minds were willing, but their legs wouldn't carry them as fast as they wanted to go. As the clock ticked down, Branko felt the fear rising in his throat. If the Selects couldn't win it in extra time, they would either win or lose in penalty kicks. And all of the pressure would be on Branko.

The Shamrocks and Selects tried to push themselves forward, but they could give no more to their causes. Passes went astray. Balls played for the strikers splashed harmlessly into puddles.

And then, finally, the referee blew the whistle. The game would be settled in penalty kicks — the cruelest way any sporting event can be decided.

Each team would pick five players to take turns shooting. The team with the most goals at the end would win the game. If the game was still tied after five shots, the teams would send up shooters one at a time — sudden death.

Brian pulled Branko over. "Look, in this mud they have to really hit the ball. If the ball rolls through the grass it'll slow down."

"Thanks, Brian."

"How's your side?"

"It hurts. But I can't think about that right now."

The referee flipped a coin and the Selects captain called "heads." The coin hit the wet ground — and the referee saw the profile of Queen Elizabeth II peering up through the grass.

"We shoot first!" said the Selects captain.

"Are you ready for this?" Brian asked Branko.

"I think so. My dad has been prepping me for this my whole life. I want to make him proud."

The referee blew the whistle and placed the ball on the penalty spot. The Calgary keeper took his place on the goal line. He danced between the posts, trying to distract the shooter.

Coach Muller had decided to put his top striker on the spot first. Start off with your best shooter, don't save him. The striker took three strides towards the ball and put his right foot down and into the ball. He hit it high, so the ball wouldn't slow in the wet grass. The ball cracked off the bottom of the crossbar and across the line.

Selects 1, Shamrocks 0.

The Shamrocks keeper walked away from the net and Branko took his place. The ball was placed on the spot and the Shamrocks left winger walked up to it.

Branko hopped up and down on the goal line. He heard his father's voice in his head: *"You don't guess. You make him guess."*

But the shooter didn't take his eyes off the ball. As soon as the referee blew the whistle, he ran towards the ball, driving through it with his left foot.

As the shooter made the run, Branko dove to his left. No good. The ball was struck with confidence, and grazed the bottom of the crossbar as it found its way into the goal.

Selects 1, Shamrocks 1.

Branko got up, trying to hide the fact that it felt like his side was on fire. He pursed his lips together and gritted his teeth. And he forced himself to jog away from the goal, despite the pain, allowing the Calgary keeper to take his place.

The Selects forward put the ball on the spot, then picked it up and put it down again. He smacked his boot behind the ball, to push some turf back into place.

Just shoot, Branko thought. *Just shoot.*

The shooter turned his back towards goal.

Oh no, Branko thought. *He's nervous. And he's showing it.*

The Selects forward turned back to face the keeper. He looked down at the ball, then up at the left side of the net. He took a final awkward step towards the ball, slipping on that same piece of turf he had tried to put back into place. The keeper dove towards his left. The Selects shooter leaned backwards as his right foot met the target, and the ball sailed high over the crossbar.

Now the pressure was squarely on Branko. He took a deep breath and jogged back to the line. Each time his foot hit the ground, pain exploded on his left side. He looked towards Calgary's next shooter, a right-footed player.

Branko grimaced. He couldn't hide it any more. But, then he heard his father's voice: *"It's not enough to just read the play. You can control the play."*

Branko decided that if he couldn't hide the injury, he'd make it work *for* him. But it meant taking a major gamble. He was pretty sure that the Shamrocks knew he was hurting — but could he fool them?

The shooter looked up at him, and Branko caught his eye. Branko quickly made his face go blank and dropped his hand to his right side — not his injured left side.

"What did I tell you?" he heard the Shamrocks

keeper cry to the shooter. "I told you he's hurt!"

Branko's eyes never left the shooter's. Would the shooter take the bait? Would the shooter — and the rest of his Calgary teammates — think that Branko was hurt on his right side, not the left?

As the shooter strode towards the ball, Branko braced himself. He dove to his right — exactly where the shooter had struck the ball. His injured left felt some of the impact, but his healthy right side took the full force of the fall. Branko stayed focused on the ball as he slid across the wet grass, and got his palms to it to make the save.

Selects 1, Shamrocks 1.

The Selects right-winger was up next. As soon as he put the ball down, he looked to the referee to blow the whistle. When it came, the shooter wasted no time; he took three quick steps to the ball and shot, never once looking up at the keeper. The keeper went left, the shot went right, and the ball nestled in the back of the net.

Selects 2, Shamrocks 1.

Branko walked back to the goal. The Shamrocks' big defender put the ball down on the spot. He had a hard, powerful shot.

I bet he's going to try and put it right through me, thought Branko.

Branko dipped his right shoulder down, ever so slightly. Would the shooter bite? Would he pick up the subtle hint?

Branko watched the shooter's eyes. The shooter looked away.

I've got him, Branko thought.

The shooter moved towards the ball. Branko leaned to the right, but he had no intention of moving. Josip had warned him that the shooters with the most powerful shots often send them right up the middle. By making the shooter think he was going to dive right, Branko was hoping to increase the chance that he would kick the ball straight to him.

It worked. CRACK! The ball came fast, but it came right at him. He put his arms together and pushed the ball away.

After three rounds, it was still 2–1 for the Selects.

The Selects' attacking midfielder strode to the penalty area. He put the ball on the spot, then looked up to the goal, studying it for just a second. Then his head went back down and he ran towards the ball.

Good, thought Branko. *Don't stand over the ball. Don't give the keeper a chance to figure you out.*

The keeper dove right — and the midfielder's shot went right down the middle.

Selects 3, Shamrocks 1.

Branko felt all eyes turning to him. His team was winning. He heard cheers from the fans as he trudged through the mud back to his spot on the goal line. But his teammates said nothing. If Branko stopped this shot, the Selects would win the game after just four rounds.

They wouldn't need a fifth round because Selects would keep a two-goal lead. If Branko made this save, there was no way the Shamrocks could come back.

The shooter put the ball down. He didn't look at Branko.

Branko took a deep breath. *Think it through*. The Calgary bench knew he was trying to hide an injury, but they thought the injury was on the right side. The shooter knew Branko would *expect* him to shoot right.

So he would shoot left. Branko *knew* it. He felt it in his gut. Branko steeled himself for the pain that would explode against his injured ribs.

The ball went off the shooter's foot. To Branko, it looked like it was a beach ball that was headed towards him in slow motion. Branko leaped to his left and stretched out his hands, and the ball didn't even sting as it hit his fingers. The pain that shot through his side as he landed drowned out the joyful roar of his teammates and the applause of the crowd. But Branko didn't care about that. He had won the championship game! He looked to the stands, and looked his father in the eyes.

Josip stood up and clapped, with his hands above his head. He grinned down at Branko. And Branko smiled back.

"It's a good thing it's raining," Josip said to Frank, who was sitting beside him. "Good thing it's raining, because I don't want Branko to see his old man's tears."

16 HOMECOMING

"Dad, why did you stop here?" Branko and Josip had been on the road for just over three hours, making their way back home from Calgary. But Josip had pulled over in the parking lot of a north Edmonton strip mall. He'd gotten out of the truck to make a phone call.

Now Branko watched his father in the parking lot, cell phone pressed to his ear. He nodded a couple of times, then ended the call and put the phone into his pocket. He walked back to the cab, got in, and turned the key in the ignition, firing the engine back to life.

"Sorry, son. Forgot that I had to make that call. It's about work."

"Okay, Dad," Branko said. "It's six p.m. on a Sunday night, and for some reason you have to call the grain elevator?"

"Yes," Josip said as he pulled out onto the St. Albert Trail and headed north towards Morinville. "Branko, did you hear that the Pelletiers are back in town from Brandon?" Josip asked.

"Why?"

"Guess their junior team had an exhibition game in Edmonton over the weekend."

"So?" said Branko, his eyebrow raised. "What does that have to do with anything?" Branko turned to look at the backseat, where his Most Valuable Player trophy sat. He felt the rush of pride he'd experienced when he had been named the league's MVP — and then he sighed. "It just means that when we get back to town everyone's going to be talking about the Pelletiers. So, nothing changes."

Josip laughed so hard that he almost pulled the truck off the road.

"Dad?"

"Nothing, Branko," Josip said, taking a hand off the steering wheel to wipe a tear from his eye.

Another half-hour passed and Branko felt relieved to see the familiar buildings of Morinville. He couldn't wait to get home and crawl into bed. Then Branko realized that his father had turned on the right-turn signal, even though they should have been going straight down 100 Avenue to get to their house.

"Dad, where are we going?"

"I have to make one other stop."

"What? Dad. It's been a long day."

"*Shh.* Branko. One more stop. Just an errand I have to run."

Why is Dad acting so strange? Branko thought.

The pickup made a right turn, then zipped into the Morinville arena's parking lot.

"Why are we going to the arena?" Branko asked. "And, wait, why is this parking lot full?"

It was true. There wasn't a stall to be found. Wait. There was one stall. Right by the arena doors — one free spot. A sign was taped to the wall in front of the parking spot. "Reserved. VIP."

Josip pulled into the spot and honked his horn.

"Dad? What are you doing?"

"Son. Just get out of the car. Oh, and bring the MVP trophy with you."

Branko crossed his arms and refused to undo his seat belt. "Look, Dad, I'm not going anywhere till you tell me what's going on. My ribs are sore and I want to go home and rest."

"You can rest — soon. But, for now, just come with me and bring the trophy."

Branko sighed. *This must have something to do with the Pelletiers, since they're in town tonight,* he thought. Branko undid his seat belt and put his right hand on the trophy, pulling it out of the cab. He walked with his father over to the front entrance. A sign was placed over it: "Welcome home!"

Ugh, thought Branko. *So this MUST be for the Pelletiers.*

Josip reached for the door handle, but Scottie was already there to hold it open.

"Come in, come in!" Scottie hissed.

Branko looked at him in surprise, and Scottie laughed. "My dad and I drove all the way back here without stopping to make sure we beat you home. I wrote the story on my laptop as we were driving. I posted it to the website when we got a wi-fi connection on the road going through Red Deer."

Branko walked in with his father and Scottie in tow. He pushed open the doors to the rink and saw that the stands were full. A sudden roar came up from the crowd and it was oh, so loud. And then a rhythmic chant began: *Ann-goooh . . . ann-goooh . . . ann-goooh.*

Wait! That chant! It was *Brannn-koooo, Brannn-koooo!*

A banner was held up at the far end of the arena by a group of fans: "Soccer star — Soccer CHAMP!"

Branko looked back towards Scottie.

Scottie laughed. "See, Branko? I told you people read those stories!"

Branko spoke to Scottie, but couldn't take his eyes off the crowd. "Wow. I can't believe it. I had no idea there were so many people in Morinville who cared about soccer."

Scottie grabbed Branko's right arm and pulled it into the air. "This is how you wave to the crowd."

"Sorry, I'm not really used to this."

Branko recognized many of the faces in the crowd; he'd seen these families at the supermarket or at Warriors' games. He saw many of his G.H. Primeau classmates. And then he watched his father move to a front-row seat that had been reserved for him. But his dad didn't sit down. He stood and clapped with the rest of the fans. He watched his dad accept some handshakes and hugs from fans in his row.

Branko held the trophy up over his head. It was what the hockey players did, right? And when he heard the crowd roar, he knew he'd done the right thing.

After the mayor had said a few words, Branko saw a line form down the stairs from the stands towards his spot on the floor. He realized that if he had to shake the hand of every person in town, he'd be there all night. And his ribs were starting to throb again.

"This is the way it's done," Branko heard someone next to him say. It was Rejean Pelletier, standing with his brother. "Wave to the crowd. Make them feel like you love them as much as they love you. If you do that, then they aren't mad when you can't shake every hand or sign every autograph."

"Why don't you wave along with me?" asked Branko.

It was Ronnie, not Rejean, who spoke up. "No way, man. This is yours. You earned this. You don't need to share this with anyone."

"You played a great game against Calgary," said Rejean. "We saw all your saves online — the paper already posted the video of the penalty shootout on its website."

"Yeah, it's too bad you don't play hockey," said

Ronnie. "You'd be an animal. Maybe one day we can get you out on the ice and see how you do."

"Yeah, right!" laughed Branko. "I'd like to see you try to get a shot a past me."

Branko looked up to the rafters, at the Morinville Warriors banners hanging from the roof of the arena. They actually did look kind of nice.

"Hey," said Branko. "I don't think I ever told you guys congratulations. I watched your championship game on TV. You guys were amazing."

"I know," Ronnie said, grinning.

"Okay," Rejean whispered into Branko's ear. "Smile, wave, raise the trophy one more time. Then you can slowly turn around and then head home."

But Branko didn't turn around right away. He wasn't quite ready for the night to end. Yes, his ribs were throbbing, but he wanted to hold on for just another minute.

17 MORINVILLE REUNION

Branko couldn't believe it. Four shots. And all of them had gone past him. One had gone under the bar. Another two had gone off the post and in. And this last one had gone right through his legs.

And the shots weren't even that hard! He guessed that the shooter was deliberately taking it easy.

Ting! Another orange ball off the post and in.

"Well, at least you're staying on your feet!" laughed Ronnie as he ran to the middle of the gym to retrieve another ball.

"It's not easy," Branko said, pulling the mask up off his face. "I mean, you have to move from side to side with these pads on. I can't imagine what that's like in skates. And you have flop down, then stand up, then crouch . . . I thought it would be just like soccer goal-keeping but easier, because the net is so much smaller. But I'm awful at this. You have to promise me that next summer you'll let me take you both to that soccer field behind the school and stare you down when you try to take penalty kicks on me. I'll have the last laugh."

The Pelletiers were back home; their junior league was on its Christmas break, so the brothers got a couple of days off. They had returned to Morinville to be with their family and friends.

After his ribs had healed, Branko had surprised everyone by showing up to the high-school gym, not to practise with his dad, but to join the regular ball-hockey game. He used some of his allowance to buy some foam floor-hockey pads and a goalie stick at the local hardware store, and found an old baseball glove to use on his catching hand.

To play ball hockey, he'd had to ask for special permission from FC Edmonton. After the provincial championships, the pro team had asked Branko to join its academy, where it brought together the most talented teenaged soccer players in the province to learn from the best coaches in the area. Usually, a professional team wouldn't allow a prospect to play any other contact sport or engage in risky behaviour that could affect his performance. Branko wasn't allowed to ski or get on a snowmobile, for example. But because Branko was such a novice in ball hockey and because the league was only recreational, FC Edmonton's coaches felt that there was no way he'd seriously hurt himself. So he was allowed to play once a week.

And when the Pelletiers got back to Morinville, they couldn't resist the chance to test Branko's skills.

Their junior team in Brandon would not have allowed them to play in a full pick-up game, but no one would frown upon the Pelletiers taking a few shots on Branko afterwards.

Rejean came down the floor and flicked the ball at the goal. Branko closed his pads together and heard the thud of the ball hitting his right pad. He had stopped it!

There was a round of applause from Brian and Scottie, who were watching the action. Scottie was shooting photos. This would make for a great New Year's feature for the local paper — "Soccer Star Peppered by Hockey Phenoms!" Brian was still working to build back the strength he needed to play in goal again. He wasn't at the point where he'd feel comfortable joining a game of either soccer or ball hockey, but there was no way he was going to turn down an invite to come up to Morinville to see the Pelletiers take shots on Branko. This would be a story he could tell for years.

"You're a hockey natural!" Rejean laughed. "Maybe next year you'll try out for the Warriors. Or maybe not!"

Branko laughed. "Yeah, right. I stop one shot for every ten I let in. The scouts will be knocking at my door any time!"

Branko walked towards the bench where Brian and Scottie were sitting. He packed up his pads and mask in a large hockey bag and slung it over his shoulder.

"So you're gonna join us at Branko's for lunch?" Brian asked Rejean.

"Yeah," said Rejean. "You gonna let us take a few shots on you next time?"

"Definitely," Brian laughed. "I know I could do better than this guy." He slapped Branko on the back.

Branko, Scottie, Brian, and the Pelletiers left the gym and began the walk back to Branko's house. They came to the spot by the high school where Ronnie used to torment the junior-high kids.

"Here's your spot," said Branko. "Wanna give any of us a snow job?"

Ronnie smiled, but his cheeks were red. And not from the cold — from embarrassment.

"He's not going to say he's sorry," said Rejean. "But that look says it all, doesn't it?"

They arrived at the front door of the Stimac house. Josip and Frank sat in the living room and waved to the boys as they walked past, heading up to Branko's room.

"My dad says that your dad is taking you to Europe," said Brian to Branko.

"Yeah, just for a couple of weeks. My grandfather wanted us to come for a month, but we didn't have enough time with next year's soccer schedule," said Branko. "But we are going to Croatia. I can't wait to see it."

"And sign a contract there," laughed Brian, as he entered Branko's room.

"Not with any hockey team, that's for sure," said Ronnie.

"No, just to visit," said Branko. "The head coach over at FC Edmonton said he thinks if I have a great season next year, I might catch the eye of the Canadian Under-17 team. But that's a big if. He says there's lots I have to work on. My dad agrees, of course."

"Cool," said Ronnie. "We're hoping to make the national junior team next season."

"Man, am I going to be busy," Scottie shook his head. "Our sports section is going to be more packed than the Edmonton paper."

Branko opened the door to his room, and Brian's eyes went wide. Yes, the Osijek scarf was still there, and so was the picture of the 1998 World Cup Croatian team. But there was a huge poster of Enrique Salas over the desk, wearing a Canadian jersey. And a Canadian national team scarf was resting on the back of the chair.

"Remember when you asked me who I'd play for, Brian?" said Branko. "Canada or Croatia? If I had the choice? Well, I have an answer for you now."

ACKNOWLEDGEMENTS

Over the years I have had the chance to meet, interview, and profile many of the players who provided inspiration for this book; players who were born outside of Canada but who have made this country their home. A big shout of "Go Canada!" to Milan Borjan, Mozzi Gyorio, Simeon Jackson, and Tomer Chencinski.

Thanks to FC Edmonton, including Tom Fath and Andreas Morse, for allowing me to use the club's name in this book. Their support is appreciated.

I would also like to thank the Canadian Soccer Association, including Richard Scott, Max Bell, and Michele Dion, for their help over the years.

And thanks to my editor, Alison Kooistra, for her honest feedback and enthusiasm for this project.

MONTVILLE TWP. PUBLIC LIBRARY
90 HORSENECK ROAD
MONTVILLE, N.J. 07045